Agents of Angels (Book 3)
The Light of All

Treena Wynes

CHAPTER ––––––––1

Diamond tipped her head back and swallowed a glass of Hennessey. It burnt on the way down but felt warm and satisfying as it reached the pit of her stomach. Her vision blurred.

Outside the bar, she could hear a commotion: the unmistakable shouting of Vipers as they gave their orders. But she didn't have to think about that in here. She was a nobody, just like the other five miserable people hunched over the bar top. Nobody was talking.

"That'll be eighteen dollars," the barman said.

"I'm sure it was seventeen yesterday," said Diamond.

"Everyone's drinking and no one's making any new stock. Either prices go up, or I close down and turn you all out onto the street."

Diamond didn't argue. The barman could have said any price at all and she would have paid it. Money didn't mean anything, anymore. Not with the world ending.

The news flickered on the television set that they had in the bar. None of the broadcasts were the same as they used to be. Back before all hell broke loose, people used to complain about the news being right-wing or left-wing. Now it all had one agenda—fall in line or suffer the consequences. Every channel showed blurry footage of machine-gun-wielding soldiers marching into cities, rounding up half-angels.

"Lucifer's Agents have triumphantly captured the East Coast," the proud voice-over said. "There was little resistance from humanity, who have made the wise choice to kneel before their new infernal masters."

"Can't you turn that off?" Diamond grumbled.

"No," said the barman. "Guards will be in here at some point tonight. If they see I've turned off the official news channels they're going to have questions for me. I suggest you keep your mouth shut, miss."

Keep my mouth shut, Diamond told herself. There would have been a time when she would have punched a guy for telling her to do that. Now she was more than happy to oblige.

The fight was over. After the doorway opened, she'd tried to look for her friends, but they were nowhere to be seen. They were almost certainly dead, and more demons were coming through the portal every day. Diamond was spending her apocalypse drinking on her own in a bar. *So predictable*, she thought, as she ordered another whiskey.

As the barman predicted, a squad of heavily armed agents appeared not 10 minutes later. They kicked down the front door as though they expected a hoard of half-angels to be waiting on the other side.

Two stood guarding the door as two more entered. One was a blond man with a cold and ruthless expression. The other was an older woman with a darker complexion. She did not look particularly cruel, but Lucifer's Guards were recruiting all sorts, these days.

The blond man pointed the end of his rifle around the room. Everyone in the bar was used to this. They put their drinks down and raised their hands. The place fell silent, except for the blaring, triumphant tones of the television broadcast.

"Routine inspection," said the blond agent. "Have your identification ready."

The two agents went around the room one by one, checking IDs. Diamond hoped that the woman would check her side of the room, but it was the blond, angry-looking dude who approached her. He took her ID and stared at it intently like he might unlock some hidden secret just by glaring at it.

"Name," he demanded.

"Diamond," she said. "It's written right in front of you."

He raised his gun at her. "Don't get smart with me. I've got the infernal authority to kill."

Diamond sipped her drink. It was best to play it cool around these people. There was a time when she would have been freaked out at having a gun pointed at her face. Now it was just another Tuesday.

"Are you a half-angel?" the agent asked.

"No."

"Do you know any half-angels?"

"No."

"You understand that any knowledge withheld from guards will result in death?"

"Yes."

The guard grunted. Diamond was used to their rapid-fire questioning style. Some people bent under the pressure pretty much straight away. She had learned you had to answer quickly and sound sure if you wanted to avoid being tested. The guard lowered his gun.

"You stink of alcohol and regret," he said. "Clean yourself up. It's embarrassing."

"Sure. Right after this drink, sir."

The man grunted at her and resumed his checks. Diamond's heart was beating pretty fast, but she knew no one would be able to tell from looking at her. She kept her eyes on the TV and her mouth around her drink. Eventually, the whole bar was checked. The blond agent gave the room one last sweeping glance from where he stood at the entrance.

"Clear for tonight," he said. "You can expect us again tomorrow. Agent Ida, let's move out."

The other guard stood in the back of the room, looking serious. "I'm going to carry out some more checks," she said. "A lot of these people look scared to me. Maybe they've got something to hide."

"We've got other addresses to check, agent."

"Then get moving. I'll catch up with you."

The blond guy didn't look happy about it, but he left. The air in the bar changed. The tension ramped up another level, and Diamond could smell the fear and sweat building up on people's foreheads in the packed space. The woman walked down the center of the room, her boots squeaking with every step.

Diamond had a twist in her gut. The agents never normally lingered, and the woman was walking towards her.

Go somewhere else, she willed. *Someone else. I'm just drinking. I'm no one.*

The agent stopped. Diamond could feel the heat coming from her body. She had stopped just inches behind Diamond's bar stool.

"Miss Diamond," the agent said. "My name is Ida. You and I need to talk."

Diamond's hands started to shake, despite herself. Even so, she kept her exterior cool. She kept on sipping at her drink, and she stood as calmly as she could. "Sure," she said. "I'd love to chat."

*

Ida took her to a booth in the corner of the bar. For a long time, she didn't say anything, which was torture. Diamond tried to look casual, but this wasn't normal behavior for a guard. Normally they did their questioning out in the open. They sat in silence until the bar started to relax. People went back to their drinks and muttered conversations.

"Diamond," she said, eventually. "I'm a guard, but I'm not here to question you. I was a preacher before the hell spawn took over. I'm inside Lucifer's Guards because I'm trying to look for a way to bring it down."

"This is a new strategy," said Diamond. "Forgive me if I don't believe a word that comes out of your mouth."

"I know you're a half-angel. If I wanted to arrest you, you'd be out on the street by now."

Diamond looked around the bar to see if anyone heard what Ida had said. Then she scowled. "I don't know what you think you heard, but it's garbage. I'm just a woman having a drink, waiting for the end like everyone else."

"I've spoken to your friends. Lucas, Marco, and Mrs. Delphine are alive. They're being guarded, but I think we can save them if we work together."

Diamond scanned Ida's face. If she was lying, then what would be the point? Real guards didn't play games. They found threats and they eliminated them.

Which meant maybe this woman was telling the truth. Hearing her friends' names was like having an old wound reopened. "If they're alive, then it's hopeless. You know that."

"None of them have given up hope."

"Then they're idiots. They're going to be killed. They might as well tell the demons everything they know and speed things up a bit. Have a drink, Ida. Make yourself numb. Take it from me, you're fighting a losing battle here."

Ida turned up her nose like she was disgusted. "They were worried you might have gone back to drinking."

Diamond stood up. "Tell them to worry about themselves," she said. "Nice to meet you, Ida. I don't expect to see you again."

"You're a coward."

"I am now. It's the smart thing to be. I tried to fight. It doesn't work."

Diamond left her alone at the table. She went back to her spot on the bar and ordered another drink, using the last few notes she had to pay for it. She kept her eyes fixed firmly forward until she heard Ida stand and leave the bar.

Diamond found herself on the brink of tears, but another whiskey helped to numb the feeling. Tears weren't helpful. They only drew attention, and she wyas a nobody now. She had to start acting like it.

*

Marco leaned against the wall of his cell and closed his eyes. He could still picture Diamond's face. He'd never known anyone so fierce. When Diamond fought, it gave him hope. There had to be other half-angels out there just like her. If they bound together, then they might have a chance.

Hope was just about the only thing he had left. A small flame of it burned in his heart from the moment he got captured. Every day he had to work on that little flame, keeping it burning. Nothing ever changed in the cells and there was no news of the outside world. Without anything else to go on, hope was all he had left.

Across from him, Lucas stared, with pursed lips. The man's rounded face had thinned over their months of capture. His eyes had gone dull like he was someone else entirely.

"I can see your aura," Lucas whispered. "You have to stop being so hopeful. It'll only make the disappointment feel worse when it finally comes."

"Talking, mortals?"

Marco looked down at his feet. It was a demon who had spoken. A creature that stood eight feet tall, with a scaled, green-eyed face. Its body was a vague outline of shadow and fire. It could move silently when it wanted. Marco would never have dared to talk if he had known that it was watching.

It bent right down to the bars of the cell, placing its face just inches from Marco's. Marco could smell rotten meat on its breath. Its hunger was obvious in the way it breathed. The way it tasted the air with its tongue every few seconds. The demon chuckled at Marco's pale face. It was a hideous noise: a cruel, rasping series of outbreaths.

"Mortals who think they can talk," it said. "Mortals who think I can't see. Mortals who want to be playthings."

Marco remained silent.

"They have secrets, but they don't tell. Your secrets are keeping you alive, but I'm getting bored of trying to get them."

It opened its mouth wide enough for Marco to see rows of yellow, pointed teeth. Teeth built for ripping flesh.

The door to the room burst open. Two guards marched in and saluted the demon. The demon, mercifully, turned its attention away from the cage to address them. Marco chanced a glance at the door, and his heart lightened.

One of the agents was Ida. If she was back, then it meant one of two things. Either she had found Diamond and convinced her to help, or she'd failed.

"Any new arrivals, guard?" the demon asked.

"Three," said Ida. "They're being taken down for questioning."

"Then I'd best greet them. I'm sure they'll want to see a friendly face." The demon did its horrible laugh again.

Ida marched past, her face hard, betraying none of her true thoughts. Subtly, as she passed by their cage, she signaled to Marco. A thumb pointed downwards. A no.

Marco looked up at his friends on the other side of the cage. He shook his head from side to side, barely any movement at all, but enough to send the message.

Lucas and Mrs. Delphine looked down at their feet. Marco was sure he had just seen their fires of hope flicker and die.

He couldn't help it. A single tear ran down his cheek. In a moment, the demon was there again, right at the side of the cage.

"Showing emotion, silly mortal?" the demon said. "You know the punishment for that. Open this cage, guard. I'm going to have a little word with this mortal before I meet my new friends."

Expressionless, Ida opened the cage. Marco stood without argument. He knew what was coming, and he steeled himself for it. He had grown used to the torture by now.

CHAPTER ‑‑‑‑‑‑‑‑2

Diamond left the bar feeling less drunk than she'd hoped. Every night since she'd met Ida, she'd been running low on cash. She had some savings left over in her apartment, but they were dwindling fast. She was trying to slow down on the drinks, but it just meant she was never quite hitting the level of drunk she needed to feel numb.

The streets of Minneapolis smelt like a sewer. There wasn't any trash collection anymore, and a lot more people were living outside. As she turned the collar of her coat up to keep out some of the rain, Diamond heard a shout. She turned her head and saw a line of homeless people being told to put their backs against a wall. Several guards wielding guns were there, but they didn't frighten Diamond. What frightened her was the hooded street thug standing in front of them. He had yellow eyes and a hungry smirk on his face. No doubt he was a Viper.

He stopped at one of the men in the line, putting his face inches in front of his.

"You thought you could hide," the Viper said. "You're a fool. I know an angel when I see one."

The man's breaths were coming short and fast. "I'm not. I swear I'm just living out here."

"Your friends were going to great lengths to protect you."

"But—"

The man's words were choked into silence. The Viper had him by the throat, lifting him several inches from the ground and pinning him to the wall. Diamond knew she should be running, but she found her feet cemented to the spot. She knew the strength of a Viper's grip. The man would be killed any moment now.

What are you watching for? she thought. *You're not going to step in.*

"Test his blood, boys," said the Viper.

One of the agents stepped forward, wielding a syringe. The man kicked the Viper in the chest. Two silver wings burst forth from his back, and he charged forward, striking the guard in the chest with all his weight. The guard flew backward. He struck the wall on the other side of the street headfirst, falling still at once, blood running from his skull.

In the stunned silence that followed, the half-angel tried to fly, but the Viper tackled him to the ground before he could. Fists flew. The rest of the homeless people scattered, and then the agents turned their guns on them.

Diamond managed to break out of her stunned daze just as the gunshots started ringing out. She ran as fast as she could, turning down side alleys that she knew were dangerous, but that would offer her some cover. The guards involved would be scouring the street now, questioning and testing everyone.

Diamond ran until her lungs screamed, turning in random directions. The gunshots eventually became muted, distant noises, and Diamond paused to catch her breath. She looked around.

She'd stopped in a silent alley, but filled with people. They sat shoulder to shoulder, shaking miserably in the rain. They looked at Diamond with curious, almost pleading eyes. Diamond tried not to meet any of their gazes.

"Diamond?" came a husky voice from the side of the street.

Diamond looked down, alarmed. She saw a woman cowering near a burnt-out fire. She looked several sizes smaller and more brittle than the last time Diamond had seen her. She had the pale, drawn-out face of an addict.

If her mom had been good to herself and stayed sober, maybe she wouldn't look as old and rugged as she did. Even behind the dirt and years of drinking, Diamond could still see physical characteristics of herself in her mom: the wide, searching eyes; the strong chin; and the small, rounded lips. Diamond wondered if she would end up looking the same if she didn't start taking better care of herself.

"Don't talk to me, mom," said Diamond. "I don't want anything to do with you; and, believe me, you don't want anything to do with me, either."

But Diamond's mom was already standing up. She put her arms around Diamond, and Diamond winced. The woman smelt foul, just like the streets she was living in.

"You have a place to stay, don't you, honey?" she said. "Somewhere warm?"

"For now."

"Money?"

"Money for food. Not for drugs. Please, don't ask me for money, mom."

Her mother smiled. "A place to stay, then. Don't leave me out here. They keep moving us on, pointing guns at us. I haven't got the strength to keep going from place to place anymore."

Her mom's eyes were like a child's: wide and pleading, flecked with tears. As much as Diamond found the sight of her decrepit mother pitiful, she wasn't without a heart. She hadn't tried to think about the state that she would be in after all these years. She knew it would be bad, but this was even more pathetic than she had guessed.

"Come on," said Diamond. "Just keep your mouth shut, okay? The guards are on alert tonight for anything suspicious. And you're just about the most suspicious-looking woman I've ever seen."

*

Diamond was squatting in her apartment rather than living in it. She hadn't paid rent in over two months but no one had come to ask for it. She had to guess that her landlady had either been killed or arrested, but Diamond knew the place wouldn't be safe for long. Agents were constantly seizing property in the name of Lucifer, using apartments as holding pens for the people they arrested. Hordes of desperate people also roamed apartment buildings, trying to force their way into places where they might have a roof for the night.

But Diamond's building was in a complex at the edge of town, away from the crowded areas. For now, it was a refuge, though she wasn't stupid enough to think it would last long. She put her mom on the sofa, where she passed out almost immediately. Then she boiled some water in the kettle, filling the room with hot steam. It was foolish to trust the running water these days. Demons had taken over pretty much every bit of infrastructure in the city, but they weren't interested in keeping it operational.

Diamond looked at her mother's sleeping face and tried to feel something. The woman who had raised her was barely there anymore. She was buried beneath wrinkles and sores.

She can't stay long, Diamond decided. It was too high a risk for Diamond to be associating with anyone. She was a half-angel, and eventually, someone would figure that out and kill anyone close to her.

She went to her room and took her small plastic grocery bag filled with money. She counted it up, and it barely came to two hundred dollars. If she wasn't drinking, she could make that last a month if she was careful. But she *was* drinking, and that meant she had a few days left.

Then what? She guessed she'd be like her mom. Out on the streets, begging for coins. The thought sent a shiver running down her spine that broke through the cloud of drunken numbness from her night at the bar.

She put herself to bed and tried to forget it all through sleep.

*

The next day, Diamond knew her mom had gone as soon as she opened her eyes. The apartment was still. There was no smell of the streets emanating from the living room. She took one glance at the bag of money in her open wardrobe.

It was empty. Of course, it was empty. Just like every dollar she'd been stupid enough to leave out in the open while she was growing up.

There was a note in the bag. It was written in a scrawl, barely legible.

Forgive me, it read. *I love you, Diamond.*

She wanted to feel mad, but it just never came. Her mom was her mom, and Diamond wasn't expecting her to act any differently.

But now Diamond didn't have any money. Was she any different than her mom, now? She had enough food in the cupboards to eat today, but she was already feeling itchy from sobriety. How many days was it going to be before she was out on the streets as well?

She felt the first twinge of guilt she had felt in a long time. Her stupid choices. She thought she'd gotten past them, but they'd found her again. Times had gotten hard, and she'd looked for solace at the bottom of a bottle. Just like she always did.

*

Diamond took a step out of her apartment. She didn't want to leave, but she had to find something to drink. It was early evening; the sun was going down. Typically, the city would be quiet at this time of night, but shouts echoed from every direction. A roaring noise, the sound of a helicopter flying overhead, broke the silence—a sound Diamond hadn't heard in weeks.

Something was happening. That meant she should stay inside and hide.

But her hands were shaking. She needed to drink something, and her apartment was dry.

Cautiously, she stepped down the stairs of her building. She passed lines of quivering people who eyed her hungrily.

One of them would try and get into her apartment tonight; she was sure of it.

Out on the streets, there were crowds of people moving. Lines of soldiers had groups facing brick walls, and needles were flying in and out of their necks. It was a mass testing. Diamond felt panic rising up her throat.

A car pulled up on the street next to Diamond. She tried not to look at it. Only Lucifer's Guards drove cars these days, and she had no intention of meeting their eyes.

"Get in, Diamond. You're not safe here."

She looked. It was Ida, and her face was grim. At the same time, there were shouts at the other end of the street. A guard had seen her and was pointing in her direction.

"Do you think I'm playing games here?"

Diamond swallowed. "It sure as hell doesn't look like it."

She got into the car. As soon as she closed the door, Ida accelerated at a mad pace, and they tore through the city streets, drifting past gangs of shouting guards. There were gunshots, but Ida just kept on driving. Her hands were gripping so tight on the steering wheel that they were turning pale.

"I think your cover might be blown," Diamond said.

"You didn't give me much choice," said Ida. "It doesn't matter now. The demons are ramping up their takeover. They'd find me out one way or another."

"Do you have a drink?"

"Of course not. And you're not going to have one for a long time."

Diamond stared out of the window. They were leaving the city, taking a road that ran past fields and trees. "You know there's nowhere safe to go, right?" she said.

"Unlike you, Diamond, I've kept my eye on the world outside the city. There are still a few people to trust here and there if you know where to look for them.

CHAPTER --------3

They drove for over an hour. The road took them far from the city, into deep forests where there wasn't a single other soul in sight. Diamond tried to take some deep breaths. When she didn't drink, she got annoyed. Ida had saved her. She knew that she would be arrested or dead by now if Ida hadn't picked her up. But Diamond couldn't help finding her annoying as hell.

"Can't you play some music or something?" Diamond said.

"You want to listen to hellscape radio? I'm sure they've got some great tunes on at the moment. More marching, and the sounds of people screaming."

"Surely you've got some CDs in this thing. It looks old enough."

"Nope. Try and sleep or something. We've only got an hour to go." Ida sighed. "They said you were a fiery warrior, not a bratty teen."

Diamond resisted the urge to flip her off. She knew it would only prove the woman's point if she did.

They eventually turned onto a road that didn't look like it was supposed to be accessible. It was just a dirt track with a few tire marks, overgrown in places by huge ferns and brambles. The car groaned and grumbled over every rock and bump as it wheeled down the hill.

Eventually, they pulled up at the side of a collection of houses. It looked like a village, but it was near enough falling apart. Here and there were scattered car parts and the remnants of old fires. There were also lean-tos and shanty houses that had been built here and there. Sat just inside the shelters were hard-faced men and women They looked up with alarm as the car arrived, but stayed where they were.

Instead, out of one of the houses, it was a kid who greeted them. Diamond's heart soared to see his face.

Diamond got out of the car to greet him. Even in her hungover, irritated state of mind, she couldn't help but smile to see the kid's face.

"You're alive," she said. "It's great to see you, Little Johnnie."

"It's just Johnnie now," he said.

Diamond opened her mouth to argue. He had grown up, but he was still just an eleven-year-old kid.

Then she looked Johnnie over, properly. He didn't look a lot older, physically. But he looked as though something had changed about him. His eyes were more misty and more unfocused than ever. His usually dark skin had a pale sheen to it, like he had spent weeks indoors. His hair was now long and tied back in a single braid.

She remembered when she first met him; fragile, frightened, and whimpering in the back of her car. It looked like a lot had changed since then.

"The demons have overlooked the reserve, for now," said Johnnie. "I knew you were alive, Diamond. The Heavens told me. Though I wish you would have come sooner."

"I didn't know where to find you."

"Even if you had, you wouldn't have come."

Diamond didn't argue. The kid was right, but how did he know that? He barely looked at her as he talked. He might just as well have been talking to the trees or flowers as her.

"Come on in," he said. "We haven't got a lot of time to catch up. And there is a lot to talk about."

*

Inside the house was cozy, but a little tired-looking. The ceiling had some water stains and the walls looked as though they could use a fresh lick of paint; but there was a welcoming smell of sweetgrass in the air. Johnnie led Diamond through to a lounge that had a worn leather couch in it, as well as several beanbags for guests.

Barry was sitting on the sofa. Her father looked more worn down than ever, almost matching her mom for being disheveled. His clothes had more holes in them, and his hair hung about the sides of his head in a wild mop. As Diamond entered he smiled. He didn't even have the decency to look ashamed.

"So you're wasting food on this coward," Diamond said.

"From one coward to another," said Barry. "That doesn't mean an awful lot. But I'm doing what I always do, Diamond. Surviving. I'm glad you took my advice to do the same."

"Let's save this conversation for later," said Johnnie.

"Don't listen to a word that this kid says, Diamond. He's going to try and fill your head with all kinds of nonsense."

"Later."

When Johnnie spoke, his voice had an edge to it. It was absurd really. The kid couldn't have been older than twelve, but when he spoke, it was like there were two voices pouring out of him, one more powerful and demanding than the other. It didn't matter that he was a kid. He was a medicine man.

Johnnie sat on one of the beanbags and invited Diamond and Ida to do the same. They all sat across from each other, no one really meeting each other's eye. There was another man in the room as well, with a calm, searching expression.

"I've been training to be a medicine man for a long time," said Johnnie. "For six months now I've been here with the Elders, listening to the heavens, and learning the art of energy and healing. In exchange for his position here in the reserve, Barry has been helping me to interpret visions from the heavens," said Johnnie. "I've been receiving them every day now; each one more clear and powerful than the last. There is a chance of an angelic victory. I can see it. But we cannot reach it, divided."

"Your visions didn't stop the portal from opening, Johnnie," said Diamond. "How can you even know that they're all useful?"

As Diamond spoke, the stranger stood up. "You should show respect to the medicine man," he said. "He is the youngest in history, and his visions are a gift from the heavens."

"Thank you Elder Turningball," said Johnnie, turning and nodding in the Elder's direction. "I don't believe what we heard was a lack of respect; what we see is a lack of faith."

The Elder bowed and nodded his head after glancing at Diamond.

"Diamond, we need to rescue our friends," Johnnie continued. "They are guarded by a demon. And though Barry is an angel, he has been unwilling to fight this monster. But if we can rescue Marco, then perhaps you and him together have a chance of overcoming the demon that guards them. We can rescue everyone, and we can have a chance of pulling together an alliance."

Barry smirked. "The heavens haven't told you any of that," he said. "They give you glimpses of hope. Just enough to keep you trying. But they won't commit to helping us, will they? Open your eyes, kid."

Johnnie ignored him. Instead, his eyes were fixed firmly on Diamond's. "It all rests on you helping us, Diamond," he said. "Ida has been trying to get a message to you for ages. I'm glad you've finally accepted it."

"I didn't have much of a choice," said Diamond. "Minneapolis isn't safe for anyone anymore."

"Even more reason to act then. Will you help us?"

Diamond took a deep breath. She looked at Johnnie's face, and at Ida's. Both of them looked more determined than any face that Diamond had seen in months.

Then there was her father. A man who mocked every bit of hope that came out of people's mouths. She remembered her mother as well, reduced to a wreck, lost in hopelessness.

There's either trying, or nothing, she thought.

"Fine," she said. "But I think we're going to get ourselves, and everyone else, killed."

*

They headed out right away, with Ida promising to explain in the car. It was only Ida and Diamond that left. Johnnie wouldn't be much use, and he needed to focus on his visions.

Being thrust back into the action while still nursing a hangover made Diamond's head spin. Especially with Ida's driving. They took roads out of the forest and headed back in the direction of the city, taking isolated roads that Diamond recognized all too well.

"Where are we going?" she said.

"The demons are holding prisoners in an old rehab center just outside of the city," said Ida. "Think it's called Angel's Haven, or something like that. Ironic right?"

Angel's Haven. Diamond hadn't thought about anywhere else for a long time. "Pretty ironic, yeah."

Ida raised an eyebrow, but Diamond didn't elaborate. She had a sort of pulling feeling in her gut, knowing she was heading back to the rehab center; like she was being forced back to a life that she had chosen to leave behind.

"I'm going to take you in wearing my LG uniform. Plus a visor on, in case anyone recognizes me. They might have had word from the city that I've gone AWOL, or they might not have. It shouldn't matter. I'm taking you in as a prisoner. As soon as you see the cell room, open your wings and cut open Marco's cage. Then, it's time to take out the demon."

"Take out the demon," Diamond repeated, exasperated. "Because it's as easy as that, is it?"

"Of course not. But what else can you do? There are other half-angels in there. I doubt any of them will fight, though. They've had the spirit tortured out of them."

*

They neared the facility. There was a tense moment where Ida flashed her ID at the guard outside. He waved them in without question, and they were in the parking lot of Angel's Haven.

Diamond couldn't help her mouth from falling open. The place was a warped version of how she remembered it. Barbed wire fences had been laid out surrounding the place. The walls had been graffitied with pentagrams, and here and there were stains on the white paint that looked like blood.

She couldn't put it into words. There was a looming sense of evil that emanated from the building. She had never faced a demon in its monstrous form before, but she could only guess that she was sensing the presence of one.

Ida put handcuffs on Diamond, but loose enough for her to break out of easily when she needed to. Then, at gunpoint, she marched Diamond through the reception area of the building, and out into what had once been the treatment rooms.

The walls had been knocked through, and now it was just one open space. Every corner had been filled with cells. Diamond caught the desperate eyes of several dozen prisoners as she was led through the room, right up in front of the serpentine demon that guarded the place.

The demon leaned down to smell her. Diamond felt a deep revulsion in her stomach, and almost faltered there and then. This eight-foot monster was too strong for her to tackle.

But then she glanced to her left and saw Marco in a cage. Alongside him were Mrs. Delphine and Lucas.

Her friends looked battered and bruised, and near starved. But they were smiling at her. If they could have hope and strength, then she could, too.

"Another half-blood?" the demon said. "This one's a little runt."

"I caught her trying to run from the city," said Ida.

"Did you, now? That's interesting. We heard you were running from the city as well."

Suddenly the door to the room slammed shut. Diamond turned her head. There were two Vipers on either side of the door. Ida's gun was ripped from her hands. The demon laughed.

"Traitors everywhere you look," it said. "And after all that Lucifer has granted you, mortal. I'd have thought you'd be more grateful. I suppose we'll have to find space in these cages for both of you."

"Diamond!" screamed Marco. "Now!"

Diamond acted on impulse, adrenaline rushing through her body. She opened her wings for the first time in months and charged towards Marco's cage before the demon could react. She cut through the metal with the bowed arch of her wingspan.

Marco was on his feet in seconds, his wings open and proud. They charged either side of the demon in a heartbeat and cut the Vipers down.

Then Marco and Diamond stood at the door. Diamond reached down and tossed Ida her gun. Ida cocked it and aimed it straight at the demon's heart.

The demon looked shocked for only a second; then it resumed its horrible cackling.

"Very good mortals, very good!" it said. "You caught me off guard. You won't do that again."

From its belt, it drew a sword that looked to be made of pure shadow. When it cut the air, it seemed to absorb the surrounding light. The demon charged, swinging in a mad arch, and Diamond leaped out of the way. She tried to attack the demon's back, but suddenly there were flames on the ground, a wall of heat and smoke blocking her path. The demon turned to face her, jaw unhinged and wide, fangs bared.

Marco flew overhead, charging with his wings, directing the path of his flight towards the monster's neck. At the last second, the demon moved its head out of the way. Marco's wings nicked its neck, and black blood gushed out. The demon roared, filling the whole room with the smell of its fetid breath.

Marco's misjudged flight veered off course and he hit the ground hard, skidding across the floor and crashing hard against a cell. The demon did not hesitate for a moment. It rounded its shoulders, bringing its shadow blade around in a deadly blow.

"Marco!" Diamond screamed. Time seemed to stop.

He rolled away from the blow, but couldn't dodge it entirely. The blade cut right through his wing. His scream struck Diamond's heart. It was raw, almost primal.

His wing collapsed to the ground with a pitiful *thud*. The flesh of his back that the sword had passed near had turned a mottled gray color, as though it was mortifying in a matter of seconds. Ida launched a barrage of gunfire at the demon's back, but it was no use. It didn't seem to even register pain from human weapons.

Diamond took a breath. This demon was like no other enemy they had faced. Luck wouldn't help her this time.

She turned to the nearest cell of half-angels. Ida was right. They looked broken and afraid, as though they had seen the inside of hell itself. But, whatever they had gone through while they had been imprisoned, they were still people on the inside. People who had once had everything to fight for.

"Help me," she said to them. "Please."

The demon bent over Marco, unhinging its jaw.

"Please!"

Diamond thought she caught the barest glimpse of recognition in one of the prisoner's eyes. Her thousand-yard stare seemed to focus, and she stood. Her wings extended. One by one, the other prisoners followed suit.

Diamond beat her wings and flew in a circle around the room, cutting the bars of cells as she went. The demon had been too entranced in its meal of half-angel flesh. By the time it noticed what was happening, it was too late.

It swung its sword in a wild tornado, but Diamond ducked and dove around the clumsy blows. She felt a rush like she hadn't felt in a long time. It felt good to not hide anymore. She was a half-angel. She was a slayer of the forces of hell, and she was proud of it.

When the cages were opened, there was a mass fluttering of wings. The prisoners, though weakened, attacked in a swarm. The demon was hacked to pieces, dying in a pool of black blood and desperate hissing.

When the battle was over, Diamond hurried to Marco's side. His eyes were unfocused, and he was muttering things that didn't make sense.

"Say something to me," she said. "Marco, please."

But there was nothing. Just incoherent babbling in a language she didn't understand. Diamond guessed it was his native tongue.

"You need a healer," she said. "We need to get to Johnnie."

As she stood, she realized that every other half-angel in the room was staring at her; looking at her as though she was a leader, and they were looking for her advice. "We have a car waiting outside," she said. "The weakest of you can get on board. The rest of us will fly behind."

CHAPTER --------4

The flight from Angel's Haven was like something from a dream. On either side of her, Diamond could see a small crowd of half-angels soaring over the highway. They were followed by a swarm of LGs who pursued in cars, but they were easy to take out from the air. After half-angels slashed the tires on two of the cars, the rest of the guards turned back, giving up their pursuit.

As they neared the forests around the reserve, Diamond signaled for the other half-angels to fly low and duck and weave around the trees. They could move silently when they wanted to. They reached the reserve without interruption or incident and descended in front of the safe house where Johnnie was waiting in the yard.

The people of the reserve looked at the crowd of descending half-angels with fear and reverence on their faces, but Diamond didn't have time to explain anything to them. She descended to Ida's car, where Marco was being pulled out and laid on the grass. Johnnie ran his hands around Marco's body, muttering strange chants.

The black lines on Marco's wounds decreased in intensity. His eyes closed, and he fell into a gentle sleep, his chest rising and falling.

"I can stabilize the curse, but I can't remove it," said Johnnie. "He needs rest for now, but he won't be able to fight. His life isn't going to be the same. He is lucky he is not dead, but he's going to spend his life fighting this curse."

Marco stirred. Diamond held his hand, tears running down her face. She hadn't even realized she was crying until the first warm drop fell from the end of her chin.

In all of her time wallowing in self-pity, Diamond had refused to think of Marco. The thought was just too painful; riddled with too much guilt. She hadn't even had a chance to have a conversation with him.

Johnnie put an arm on her shoulder. "You rescued him," he said. "If you hadn't broken him out he would be dead right now. You fought for him, Diamond. Don't feel guilty about that."

"That's easy to say," said Diamond.

"You're going to have to believe it. We haven't got time to mourn." Johnnie looked up to the heavens, in that detached way of his. "There is much to discuss. And we need to plan our next move. The death of a demon won't be ignored."

*

The small house in the reserve was filled with people. Many of them were prisoners. The people of the reserve handed out hot bowls of vegetable stew with crusts of bread, and they were eating hungrily. Out of all of them, only Mrs. Delphine refused a meal, even though she had just spent months inside a cell.

She was focused and fierce, despite what she must have gone through. She sat at the head of the crowd, naturally attracting the focus of every person gathered. Diamond smiled to herself. Her tenure as leader didn't last long, but she wasn't surprised. Mrs. Delphine had authority in any room she was in.

"Today we have the beginnings of a resistance," she said. "Every single person in this room achieved a victory today against a force that is larger and more powerful than us. That is something to be celebrated.

"We can expect that this breakout will not be broadcast. It will remain a secret that only the demons, Vipers, and their guards are aware of. They will ramp up their searching and testing. Our time here is short. As safe as we appear to be now, we cannot spend too much time resting. We need to act, and to plan our next move."

One of the prisoners raised a hand. Mrs. Delphine nodded her permission for her to speak.

"With all due respect, we've got our freedom now," she said. "We didn't ask to be rescued, but I'm thankful for it. That doesn't mean I want to risk my life fighting against something we can't win against."

"I understand," said Mrs. Delphine. "You are free to go where you want, of course. But ask yourself, where will you go? Where is safe for half-angels now? We don't have safety. We'll have to make it ourselves."

"There are other parts of the country we could go to," said another prisoner.

"There are. But we don't have any news that isn't filtered through the demon-controlled media. Who knows what's happening in other states? It could be worse. It could be better. But for how long?"

"What about the heavens? We're half-angels. Aren't we supposed to get some sort of divine intervention on our side?"

Mrs. Delphine deferred to Johnnie to answer that question. He might only have been a kid, but he was already being treated with a level of respect and reverence beyond his years.

"The heavens do not just send help," he said. His voice was quiet and calm, yet it carried around the room. "They need to work alongside the free will of people. And, so far, people haven't given much to prove their worth. Barely anyone has fought back since the opening of the portal. People have grappled for power, abandoning their values for their freedom and safety in a world run by demons. We may get help from above, but we need to prove ourselves yet."

*

After the meeting, Mrs. Delphine said she had to think carefully about their next move. She said she would have more direction when she had balanced the risks. No one questioned her. Everyone gathered in the reserve was a lost soul; a person desperate for direction. As long as Mrs. Delphine remained calm and assured, those people would listen to her.

Diamond waited for the lounge to clear out and then collapsed on the sofa. With the immediate danger gone and her body no longer running on adrenaline, she was feeling the strain of withdrawal more than ever. Her head was beginning to throb, and the sweat on her brow had gone cold.

"You look terrible," said Barry, entering the lounge.

"I suppose that's one thing we have in common, then."

Barry gave a little snorting laugh, then sat across from Diamond on a beanbag. He pulled a hip flask out of his pocket and gave it a swig. Diamond's mouth went dry.

"What did you think about what Johnnie said?" Barry continued.

"It gave me a bit of hope. A bit." She frowned. "I'm not in the mood to talk about this."

"If you all charge in blindly, thinking that you're going to be saved with some help from above, then you're wrong. I know you don't think I care Diamond, but I don't want you to run head-first into death."

"It's a bit too late to start caring now. Seriously—quiet. I've got a headache."

"Want a drink?"

Diamond stared at the offered flask. Barry didn't know about her alcoholism. She was sure he never would have offered if he did. Diamond knew that the answer was supposed to be "no," but it seemed to take her mouth an age to make the words. Drinking would numb all of it: the worry, the stress, the anxiety of not knowing.

But she knew she couldn't go down that path again. Not now. She shook her head. Barry shrugged and kept on drinking. For a few minutes they sat in an awkward silence: the mismatched feeling of a father and daughter, completely unaware of the circumstances of each other's lives. They should have had everything in common. They had nothing.

"I saw mom in Minneapolis," said Diamond eventually. Just to break the silence more than anything else. "She looked terrible."

"She wasn't always like that," said Barry, finishing off the last few drops of his flask.

He didn't say anything else about her. Diamond lay down on the couch.

People flitted in and out of the room. Some tried to talk to her. Diamond didn't reply. She didn't feel part of reality.

Her head was swimming, her vision fuzzy. She knew that these withdrawal symptoms would pass, and all she could do was try and suffer through them.

Eventually, Johnnie entered the room. He stood over Diamond until it felt weird ignoring him. Diamond grunted.

"Don't tell me it's time to go," she said.

"Not quite," said Johnnie. "But Marco's awake. I thought that you'd want to talk to him."

Diamond sprang to her feet at once. Her heart was suddenly beating incredibly quickly.

*

Marco had been given a place in one of the few beds that the house had. It was a small single room with barely enough space to walk through. As Diamond entered, he managed a weak smile. The wound on his side was completely wrapped in bandages.

"It's good to see your face again," he said.

"I wish I could say the same." Diamond's breathing began to come short and shallow. "I'm sorry Marco. I should have been there sooner."

"You're alive. That's all I care about."

"I abandoned you. Plus there was everything with Ty."

"I just care that you're safe."

Diamond smiled at him, and he smiled back. She reached for his hand and held it tight. It was just a fleeting moment in a storm of craziness, but holding his hand made Diamond feel calm. "You need to rest," she said. "And Mrs. Delphine is going to be telling us to move any second. Let's talk again later, okay?"

"But what about us, Diamond?"

"Now really isn't the time for that Marco."

"It never is."

Diamond sighed. It was painful. Every part of her wanted to be a teenager again, to sit down with Marco and pretend that they were the only two people in the world. But they didn't have that luxury anymore. They were living on the brink of oblivion. Now it was time to think with her head; not her heart.

CHAPTER ————————5

When Mrs. Delphine called everyone together, she had several locals from the reserve with her. They had proud, hard faces. They looked like sentinels as they stood on either side of her.

"I've spoken to the Elders here," she said. "With Johnnie and Marco's help, we've convinced them to go a step further in helping us. We are going to take into the woods and disappear for a while until we can gather our strength and come up with a plan. They are going to show us how to live in the old way, with tents, streams, and surviving on what the land provides. We're going to keep moving and keep away from the Vipers who are now going to be tracking us. Our friends' local knowledge gives us an advantage. This plan will give us breathing room so that we can be ready to regroup. Does anyone have any questions?"

Diamond looked left and right. Everyone was listening without argument. The new half-angels with them didn't seem to have an independent thought in their heads.

No one else was going to speak up, so Diamond guessed it was up to her. She cleared her throat.

"What do you want to say, Diamond?" asked Mrs. Delphine. She looked impatient, even though her voice was calm.

"It sounds like running," said Diamond. "While we're gathering our strength, more and more demons will pass through the portal. Perhaps more than ever, since we struck the first blow. We can't just wait."

"Our enemy is already far stronger than us. Attacking now won't give us an advantage."

"It's still the best chance we have."

"Does anyone else echo these concerns?"

To Diamond's surprise, Lucas stepped forward. She had never seen him disagree with Mrs. Delphine before, but his face was serious. "We have half-angels now," he said. "I don't think Diamond is saying that we take this fight straight to Minneapolis, but there must be some other target we can hit. Something small, but that will have an impact."

Mrs. Delphine pursed her lips. "I'm not going to force anyone to come with us," she said. "But we have to be one voice here. If most people agree with my plan, we leave." She turned to face the crowd of people. "A show of hands, please, for those who wish to follow me into the woods."

To Diamond's shock, only about a third of the hands in the room went up. Even the people from the reserve who Delphine had rallied for help did not fully agree with her. Diamond felt bad at once. Mrs. Delphine looked crestfallen. She sighed and sat down on the couch.

"Fine," she said. "Let's think about what targets we can hit."

*

Elder Turningball—who revealed that his first name was Jerome—provided a large, detailed map of the area. There were nothing but woodlands for miles in every direction, so they turned their attention to the areas nearest to the city. Diamond lost confidence at once. There were so many little bits of infrastructure outside of the city. Who knew which one of them would be useful to strike?

To everyone's surprise, it was Johnnie who gave a suggestion first, despite being nearly silent the rest of the day.

"We should strike this broadcast tower," he said, dreamily. He brushed the area of the map without looking at it. "This is where they send their messages from. The ones currently being shown on every single screen in Minneapolis."

"You know that for certain, do you?" asked Mrs. Delphine.

"I've been given messages in my visions."

Mrs. Delphine pursed her lips. She was still annoyed at being superseded in her decision-making, but she wasn't one to argue with Johnnie. Johnnie's word, even among the new arrivals, was already being treated with reverence.

Diamond never forgot how he had been introduced to her. It was said that he would see the end of the Great War before it finished. Though the visions that he received from the heavens were always vaguely defined, they always seemed to be a good predictor of the truth in the end.

"Did your visions give us anything we can work with?" asked Mrs. Delphine. "Do you know how many soldiers there are? How many demons? We can't just wander into somewhere with the flimsiest amount of information to work with."

"There are going to be risks, Mrs. Delphine. They're unavoidable," said Lucas.

"I thought you were smarter than this, Lucas."

"Smart isn't going to cut it anymore. We have to be bold." He put a hand on Mrs. Delphine's shoulder. "Diamond's never steered us wrong before. We've been guiding her so far, but now it's time to trust her."

Mrs. Delphine looked at his hand, and her resolve seemed to crumble. She sighed, but then she forced a hard smile on her face. It wasn't convincing, but it was something. "Alright," she said. "But we need a plan of attack that's going to reduce risk and causalities. We need to think about scouting the area, and perhaps tackling two places at once."

Diamond watched the conversation turn to tactics without really feeling as though she could contribute. She had defeated servants of hell before, but only with the help of others, and no small amount of luck. Battle tactics were beyond her.

She felt a little bit of doubt as she saw the room come to life with a raucous discussion about the plan she had come up with. It was a big decision and one that had come from her gut.

But Mrs. Delphine's doubt was hard to ignore. Sure, the woman wasn't a general, but she had been working with angels for a long time, and keeping tabs on threats from the demon world.

Perhaps her cautious approach had something to it, as well. But to hell with it. Diamond had made her choice. And, after helping to slay a demon, she was ready to get to the fight again. What they needed now were advantages. Things on their side that the enemy wouldn't be expecting.

She could only come up with one idea. And it wasn't a brilliant one.

*

With the lounge full, Barry had gone outside to drink and be miserable. He sat under a lean-to made out of corrugated metal. He stared out into the rain, looking at nothing in particular. He didn't seem to even notice Diamond's approach.

Diamond had no idea of the full extent of what the man had been through over the years, but it couldn't have been pretty. Sometimes it seemed like he was lost in a maze of his thoughts. Or maybe his head was still stuck in some painful slice of the past.

"You heard about what we've got planned?" she said, sitting down next to him.

"Didn't sound much like a plan. Sounds like you're all desperate to get yourselves killed."

"Maybe we're all going to end up that way if we don't fight."

"I know what you want. Save your breath, sweetheart."

Diamond opened her mouth, then closed it again. She couldn't think of a single point that would get the attention of her stubborn, hard-ass father. He wouldn't be moved by the idea that he might get to serve some greater good. Just one look at his disheveled hair and his thousand-yard stare and she could see that he had given up on the greater good a long time ago.

"I get it," he said, finally. "Take a look at me. You can't see me as a warrior, can you? But I was. And it cost me everything. Including my loyalty and my trust. And those things aren't easily regained."

"I don't want to watch you go through the same thing. I know I've not ever been a dad. You're well within your rights to ignore me. But if you want my advice, you should keep your head down. Let other people kill themselves."

"You know I'm not going to do that."

"And you know I'm not going to help."

"I knew before I asked."

Barry grunted, then stood suddenly. "Follow me," he said.

He took her to a back room of the main house, where most of the arrivals had dumped their belongings. (if they had any to dump). He ignored all of the bags and instead went to a locked cabinet in the back, which he opened with a crooked old key that he pulled out of his pocket.

"I put this here as soon as I arrived, and made Johnnie swear not to tell anyone about it," he said. "I have no idea why I kept this thing so long. I guess because it reminded me of what I used to be. But you'll do better with it."

He reached into the back of the cabinet and pulled out a sword. It looked rusted, with red-tinged edges and a smell like old coins. But as he held it, suddenly it came to life. It shone with silver light and became as sharp as a chef's knife.

"It's like the opposite of what that demon was holding," said Diamond.

"It's from the heavens. Probably the only thing on Earth, other than me, that's divine. Use it and fight with it, Diamond. It's just about the only bit of help I'm able to give right now."

Diamond rejoined the gathering of half-angels, people from the reserve, and other allies in the lounge. Pots of coffee had been brewed, and the place reeked of it. Fueled by caffeine they strategized well into the night. Diamond tried to get her voice heard as much as she could.

Barry asked her to keep the sword a secret, so for now, she had put it back in the cabinet. She would find a way to sneak it with her when they moved ahead. Knowing she had a heavenly blade gave her renewed confidence. It had to be an advantage, even if it was a secret one.

*

There was no rest the next day. At the crack of dawn, Mrs. Delphine had everyone grab their things and line up outside the head of the reserve. The Elders handed out survival provisions to everyone there: blankets, fire lighters, skins of water.

When everyone was kitted out, Diamond thought they looked like badasses. Like survivors.

"We can get to the radio tower by night if we keep up the pace," said Delphine. "Then we're going to camp in the woods nearby. Stanley is going to branch out and scan what's ahead and what's behind us. He'll let us know if we're seen."

"We have wounded among us, so our pace is going to be slow," she added. "Just remember to stay together. It's far more important than getting there quickly."

"You're really coming?" Diamond whispered to Marco.

He was on his feet, but lingering at the back of the ground. Johnnie stood by his side, constantly looking over his wounds. Diamond thought that he looked intoxicated. He was swaying on the spot even when he was standing still.

"It's not like I can stay here," he said.

"That little half-smile isn't very convincing."

He chuckled. They shared a smile—a real one, with warmth in it. Diamond's heart felt lighter, seeing that. Even with all the darkness they were about to face, there were things to smile about.

"About what I said in the tent," he continued. "I do want to talk about it again."

"So do I," said Diamond. "But now isn't the time."

Marco looked down at his feet, frowning. Diamond put an arm around his shoulder. It was about the best she could do, for now.

CHAPTER --------6

The walk through the woods was hard. Harder than it should have been. Diamond wanted to focus, but her mind started to drift. If it wasn't for the people around her spurring her on, she was sure the temptation would overtake her and have her searching for a drink, instead. She found herself lagging behind the others, at the very end of the trail. Even Marco was ahead of her, though now and then he was being carried on a stretcher by two of their guides from the reserve.

It was a long and grueling day. They ate just as the sun was going down: a meal of greens, mushrooms, and dried meat provided by Jerome. There was enough to eat, but it didn't make Diamond feel satisfied. She wasn't craving food, after all.

She went with a dozen others to scout out the broadcast tower. The edge of the tree line met an open field surrounded by a tall chain-link fence; the broadcast tower was just inside that. Jerome disappeared for an hour or so to try and scout further, to find out what kind of force they were up against.

Diamond waited with Mrs. Delphine and Ida. No one was talking. They all knew what they had signed up for, but now, the reality of launching an armed assault on a building was beginning to set in.

Eventually, Jerome returned. He smelled of mud and earth, and his hair was filled with pine needles. "I can see three armed guards outside," he said. "There could be more in there, but we cannot know for sure."

"That's not a lot to go off," said Mrs. Delphine.

"It's all we're going to get."

Mrs. Delphine looked pale, but she nodded. "Then we stick with the plan. Diamond, you know what you have to do?"

"I wish I didn't," said Diamond, grimly.

"We can have someone else lead the attack if you want."

Diamond drew her sword. Even in the dark of the night, it was bright and brilliant. She swung it into the wind, and air whistled on either side of the sharp edges of divine steel. "Not a chance," she said. "We attack from the air, and you guys from the ground. By the time they've figured out what's going on, it'll be too late."

"In theory."

Mrs. Delphine wasn't meeting her eye. Diamond felt a bubble of guilt in her chest.

"I'm sorry," she said. "For arguing with your decisions. I just had to do what's right."

"You think with your gut, Diamond. You always have. And Lucas was right—it's not served us wrong before. I believe in you, Diamond. I know you probably haven't heard that much in your life, but it's true. I've seen you grow from a troubled teen to the powerful young woman I see in front of me. I couldn't be prouder."

Diamond felt tears dripping down her nose before she could stop them. They were warm, and she felt her cheeks go hot at once. She never liked showing weakness in public.

Mrs. Delphine embraced Diamond in a hug. For once, Diamond let herself be vulnerable. She fell onto Mrs. Delphine's shoulder and felt the woman's hand running through her hair, giving her some comfort, despite everything.

*

Diamond looked on either side of her. Her legion of half-angels, who only the night before had been half-starved prisoners, looked fierce now. Diamond had gotten to know one of them—the first who had been prepared to fight during the rescue. Her name was Sepharius, and she had a vengeful fire in her eyes.

"Don't pull any punches," Diamond said to her.

"Don't worry about me," said Sepharius. "You just try not to cut yourself on that sword."

Diamond grinned at her. Then she turned to face the rest. "We're going to strike and fight from the roof downwards," she said. "Keep things close quarters. Sail over their gunshots. We're going to show them that angel blood isn't saintly. It isn't pure. Its unyielding power."

There were cheers of approval at Diamond's words. Sepharius made a noise that was close to a roar. There were shouts over the hill—the waiting LG soldiers overhearing them. But what the hell did it matter now?

With one mighty beat of her wings, Diamond soared higher into the air than she ever had before. The top of the broadcast tower was below her. Cold wind and rain slapped at her face but, just behind them, dawn was breaking. In the white glow of the morning sun, she pointed her sword down at the roof of the tower and charged like a bullet. With a chorus of whistles and shouts, her fellow half-angels followed suit.

People were already gathering on the roof below them, wielding chains and clubs. They had to be Vipers. No full human would risk tackling angels in a melee brawl.

But these Vipers were underestimating them. Diamond had already taken down her fair share of demon spawn, and this lot were just pawns to her now.

She landed on the roof with a roll, straight into the path of an approaching Viper. She swung her sword upwards with her as she straightened her back and her blade cut through flesh. It broke through bone like she was cutting through butter, and the Viper was severed. His body fell apart in a disgusting comedy, one half sliding from the top of the other.

Another Viper screamed, "Get the runt with the sword!" He lashed out with his chain, and Diamond jumped aside from the blow. This time she drove her blade forward like a stinger. It broke through the Viper's chest and out the other side.

The other half-angels landed on either side of her. Half-demon clashed with half-angel as they fought for the rooftop.

The half-angels had the upper hand. They attacked with airborne flurries, forcing Vipers off the side of the roof. Even as more Vipers were coming up the stairwell, they were met with crossbow bolts, fists, and Diamond's blade. For once in her life, Diamond felt invincible. With her half-angel comrades at her side, she felt like they could sweep over the forces of hell like a storm.

*

Ida took a deep breath and steadied her aim. Somewhere in the broadcast tower, there was an alarm going off. She looked on either side of her and grimaced. The folks from the reserve knew how to hold a crossbow, but some of the others—like Lucas and Mrs. Delphine—looked like kids holding toys.

The camp was about half a mile behind them, where the weird kid and Marco were. Ida reminded herself that it was the half-angels that were going to do the brunt of the fighting. Their job on the ground was to distract and divide attention and to stop any LGs from getting past them and down to the vulnerable people in the camp.

"I hear a lot of fighting," said Mrs. Delphine next to her.

"Sounds like they had more people inside than we thought." She peered through the binoculars that Jerome had given her. The top of the roof was a flurry of action, but Diamond and her half-angels looked like they were dominating.

Ida had been doubtful of Diamond. Lucas, Marco, and Mrs. Delphine had insisted that she would be just who they needed to start a fight against the hell spawn. When Ida had first met her though, all she had seen was an entitled kid who didn't have an ounce of guts in her.

She saw now how wrong she had been. Diamond was the rallying cry that brought the half-angels together. If Mrs. Delphine was their wise leader, then Diamond was their fearless general.

"Let's begin," said Mrs. Delphine.

"I don't have a clear shot," said Ida.

"You don't need to. We just need them to know that we're here."

Ida peered down the barrel of her gun, aiming at one of the guards patrolling the building. They were on alert now, scanning the perimeter of trees.

Ida let out a burst of fire that cracked violently over the hills. As she predicted, she missed her mark. But the response from the LGs was immediate.

Suddenly figures were moving down the grassy slope towards them. There were at least a dozen, and Ida swore. No wonder they weren't taking cover: They had more numbers on their side than they had known.

"Fire, dammit!" she screamed at the others.

She aimed at figure after figure with her rifle, taking them out in short bursts. A few went down, but the others kept on charging. Whatever hellish commander was leading these people, they didn't care how many guards they lost in the fray.

The sporadic single *clunks* of crossbows on either side of her slowed. Ida realized quickly that her allies were barely taking down any of the LGs approaching. They were either missing them or were hitting them in non-lethal places.

The LGs, on the other hand, were dangerously close to the mark. Ida threw herself to the ground as bullets ricocheted through the branches over her head.

"Fall back!" Ida screamed. "Follow me!"

Her voice was nearly lost over the gunfire. She turned to run and could see others on either side of her doing the same. The air reeked of smoke. Ida was smothered by sharp splinters as the tree trunks were cut into pieces.

She ran about 20 meters and took cover behind a thick trunk. She pointed the barrel of her gun around the side and aimed at the figures now entering the woods. Three went down. Running off adrenaline. she found her aim was greater than it had ever been.

For the love of God, she thought. *I used to be a preacher.*

The figures kept coming. Without help, they were going to be overwhelmed. Next to her, Mrs. Delphine was fighting valiantly, but her crossbow bullets just weren't being loaded fast enough to make a difference.

*

Diamond focused again when the last of the Vipers had been cleared from the building. She had been on a rampage, taking more lives in the last few minutes than she ever had before. Yet her sword was pristine. Blood seemed just to run off its pure white surface.

She didn't want the spell to end. They were a coordinated force of hope, and she didn't want to stop the momentum. "Let's get into that building and mess them up!" she shouted.

Sepharius was by her side, her knuckles cut and bloody. "We should go down to the ground," she said. "I hear a lot more gunshots than I was expecting."

"And risk losing the building? No."

"Listen, Diamond."

She sounded so panicked that Diamond was shaken from her focus. She listened, and she heard what sounded like a war zone; a relentless barrage of gunshots.

She looked at the trees where her friends were fighting. There were LGs—a hell of a lot of them—moving into the tree line.

"Crap," she said. "Down to the ground!"

Diamond took flight, and her other half-angels followed her.

They landed in a fury, just behind the charging soldiers. Fighting together they cut down half of them. Some turned their weapons, but not quickly enough. The half-angels were upon them, knocking them to the ground and ripping their guns from their hands.

Diamond found Ida and the others a little deeper into the woods. Ida's pupils were dilated. Her breathing was short and shallow.

"We got here just in time by the looks of it," said Diamond. "Well done, guys."

"Diamond. Please look."

She turned her head. Her mouth fell open and her world began to blur.

Mrs. Delphine was on the ground. She was sitting against a tree trunk, clutching at her breast. Blood was pumping through her clothes and out over her hands. Lucas was next to her, sobbing.

"Mrs. Delphine, please hold on," he said. "We'll get you back to camp. Johnnie can help to heal you!"

But it was too late. Mrs. Delphine, their trusted leader, went limp. She fell to the ground with her eyes shut tight.

CHAPTER --------7

Mrs. Delphine's body was looked after by the people from the reserve. They chanted in their traditional language as they laid her to rest upon the grass, just beyond the woods where she had been shot.

Diamond had to get away. She couldn't look at the body of her dead friend, and mentor, without guilt twisting in her stomach.

This had been *her* idea. She'd been reckless, and it had gotten someone killed.

Maybe you should have just stayed in that damned bar, she thought. *You would have been less of a risk to people.*

Almost as bad as seeing Mrs. Delphine, was seeing Lucas. Lucas had known her for longer than anybody, and Diamond had barely had a chance to say a handful of words to him since she had been back with him.

Lucas wept as if he had lost a parent. Diamond wanted to comfort him and help him calm down, but she couldn't find the right words.

Then Ida put a hand on her shoulder.

"Let's finish what we came here to do," Ida said. "If we don't take that tower, then it will all have been for nothing."

"You go," said Diamond. She sat in the grass, retracting her wings and burying her face in her hands. "I don't know what I'm doing."

"Your half-angels need to see you acting, Diamond. You've made yourself someone that they follow. They need to see their leader marking a victory."

Ida looked serious. Diamond wanted to disappear, but she knew that Ida was right. The other half-angels hadn't known Mrs. Delphine like Diamond had.

If Diamond fell into despair, then her allies would, too. They needed to keep fighting.

*

The broadcast tower had been emptied of Vipers and guards. There were a few others—sound engineers and workers who said that they had been put to work forcibly—projecting the propaganda into the local airwaves. Diamond approached one of them, a serious-looking woman who announced herself as the tower director.

"We need to send a message out right away," said Diamond. "Before they can cut it off. Everyone in the city is going to be watching."

"We'll make it happen," said the director.

Diamond waited for someone else to volunteer to be part of the broadcast. They hadn't prepared anything, and she wasn't one for throwing her face out there. But no one else offered. Ida, Sepharius, and everyone else were staring at Diamond as though waiting for her to give the call.

It didn't matter anymore that she was nervous. Someone had to act. She would have to speak from the heart.

She stepped in front of a camera, which was pointed towards a green screen. Her hoody was still wet with blood and she was still holding her sword. The studio was silent. The light on the camera turned on, and the director raised a hand, signaling that they were live.

Diamond extended her wings. This was no time to shy away from what she was.

"People of Minneapolis," she said. "My name is Diamond. My allies and I have taken control of this broadcast. We've fought Vipers, Lucifer's Guards, and we've slain a demon, as well. You need to know that we can fight back. We need to stand together for humanity.

"We are stationed here at the broadcast tower outside of the city. Look on a map and you'll see it. We intend to fortify ourselves here and plan our final stand. If any of you want to return to a life of freedom and fairness, then we urge you to join us here. Bring weapons. Bring courage. We have to fight for the world we once had."

She stepped away from the camera. The broadcast ended.

Diamond shared a hard, meaningful look with Ida. This was it, now. They had announced themselves, and Diamond had shown her face. There wouldn't be any turning back.

It was time for the future, or it was time for destruction.

*

The grisly process of dealing with the bodies wasn't something that anyone there had experience in. Burying seemed the respectful thing to do, but the thought of all that labor and time spent out in the open didn't seem all that smart. Especially now that they had announced themselves. Who knew when a counterattack was coming? They needed to be inside the tower, using it like a fortress. Marco, Johnnie, Barry, and the others were brought up from the nearby camp.

Instead, they worked together to build a fire. The bodies of the Vipers and LGs were burnt in a heap, and the sickly sweet smell of crackling fat made Diamond gag.

They took the time to bury Mrs. Delphine. Lucas tried to say a few words, but they kept getting caught in his throat as he broke out in sobs. In the end, Marco had to step in. He had taken the news with grim acceptance and was holding his own better than anyone.

"Mrs. Delphine was our leader," he said simply. "But to some of us, she was more like a mother. Not everyone gathered here today knew her well. Just know this was a huge loss. But it's one we can recover from if we stick together."

Diamond could barely stand to watch. Guilt felt like poison coursing through her body, threatening to drive her mad. She went back up to the roof of the broadcast tower to find some peace and catch her breath. She sat down and leaned against the stem of the radar dish, burying her face in her hands.

"You want to be alone?"

Diamond looked up. Lucas was there. His blond mop was plastered to his head with sweat. His eyes looked red and raw from crying.

"I'm sorry," Diamond said. "This is all my fault."

"Your fault? Diamond, you and your half-angels saved lives out there. And don't forget, I was just as supportive of your plan as you were. Only our enemies can be blamed for this."

"No. We should have been more cautious."

"Maybe. Or we might *all* be dead by now if we were. We can't sit on what might have been, Diamond. It isn't a luxury that we have right now."

He sat down next to her and held her hand gently. Diamond squeezed it back and forced a smile. It felt good to be in Lucas' company. Lucas had been there from the beginning, after all. He had been the one to introduce Diamond to all of this craziness, and he'd always supported her, even when times were hard.

"Sorry we haven't talked much," he said. "It's been a roller coaster since you've come back. It's probably for the best, though. I'm not sure how long I could have stayed locked up for, without losing my mind."

"I was being selfish then, as well."

"You're human, Diamond. As well as half-angel. Humans make mistakes. Especially when they're up against something like this." He nodded towards the city. Minneapolis lay not far from them. There were still helicopters overhead; even fires, in places. "Down there is a city filled with people who have rolled over and taken everything that the demons offered them. At least you're trying to do something about it."

"It would be easier if we had help."

"Your broadcast will help. People will come."

"And if they don't?" She sighed. "I'm beginning to see what Barry means. We're out here sacrificing our lives to fight off demons, Vipers, and anyone stupid enough to follow them. Where are the other half-angels? How much can they ignore before they're willing to be involved?"

"We can talk to Johnnie about it tomorrow," said Lucas. "For now, let's just grieve. We might not get another chance."

So they did. They spent the evening sharing stories about Mrs. Delphine. They laughed and cried. By the time the sun came up, Diamond did feel a little better.

CHAPTER --------8

The day was filled with action. Gates were locked, and guards were put out on the same watchtowers that the LGs had been using. With the tower directors' help, they dragged tables, sandbags, filled trash bags—everything that they could find—and built barricades across the land surrounding the tower.

The assault weapons that the LGs had wielded were handed out to those who were the best shot and therefore could make the most use of them. Half-angels took turns carrying out flying sweeps of the perimeter, making sure there was no approaching retaliation, and looking out for potential allies responding to Diamond's call.

It had stopped raining for once. The little bit of warmth on their backs was brightening the mood in camp, despite everything that had happened. People worked diligently, and even joked and laughed as they did.

By the time Diamond was able to talk to Johnnie, the noon sun was high in the sky. He sat cross-legged in the grass, seemingly staring at nothing. Diamond asked him to contact the heavens, and his expression did not change.

"I can try," he said. "They may not answer."

"No one cares, then. They're leaving us to our fate."

"They are giving us a choice. Free will is the greatest gift that we have as people, and we shouldn't scorn it."

"Free will is getting us killed."

"Then perhaps people are making the wrong choices."

"Johnnie, please."

The kid turned to look at her again. For a second, Diamond saw the old Johnnie in his eyes; from before he had become all dissociated and weird. "I can try," he said again. "That's all I can offer. But we have to do it right."

*

Johnnie arranged for a traditional shelter to be put together out on the grass. The people from the reserve put it together in no time at all, moving branches and putting them together in a dome-shaped shelter. Then they covered the outside with leaves and bracken and covered the whole structure in animal skins.

It had an opening at the top, and Johnnie built a fire inside. He invited Diamond in to sit with him. As well as Barry, so that he could interpret the messages that he received.

"Jeezus it's hot in here," said Diamond as she sat.

"You get used to it," said Barry. "He always insists on doing things like this."

"The traditional way is best," said Johnnie, not taking his eyes off the fire he was building. "It helps to bring clarity and focus. Though that gets a lot harder if you don't shut up."

Barry shot Diamond a withering look that projected exactly how tired he was of these rituals.

"Let's shut up and hurry up, then," said Diamond.

Johnnie brought out a pouch filled with sage and tobacco, which he crumbled up with his hands before dropping them into the fire. The tent filled with a deep, dank, herbal smell that made Diamond lightheaded and sleepy.

"Hear me," said Johnnie. "Spirits and ancestors of the astral plain that White people call heaven." Diamond suspected the last bit was for her benefit. "We come to you now with longing and hope in our hearts. We have had a victory here and we want to have many more. What we need now is guidance, and whatever help you can offer."

"Right," said Barry. "Because they've been so forthcoming so far."

"Shut up," hissed Diamond. She was spellbound by Johnnie's words. When he spoke it was at a pitch and frequency that she wasn't sure she'd be able to recreate. It was high and low in places and had a strangely melodic hum to it.

It was clear that he was talking to two realities at once. His words were reaching places that no normal voice could. It was odd.

In all of the time that Diamond had realized that she was a half-angel, she had many experiences that had put her in touch with the voices and creatures of hell. But, beyond her connection to her father, she had had very little contact with the heavens. She was part of it, but it had never taken notice of her—or so it seemed. How was that possible?

The air went still. The fire in the room suddenly shrank down into nothing. Diamond started, but Johnnie signaled for her to settle.

The wind stopped. There was silence in the tent.

For what seemed like an age, the three of them sat in silence. Diamond looked across at Johnnie's face, which was tight and twisted in concentration. She looked at Barry's face. He looked bored; like he had been through this countless times before.

There was suddenly a fluttering of wings. Johnnie took them outside. Diamond expected to see an angel descending towards them.

But it wasn't an angel; it was an eagle. It beat its wings with force as it lowered itself towards the ground. Then it settled there on the grass, looking up at each of them expectantly.

"What's going on?" said Diamond. "What do we do now?"

"In their ceaselessly dramatic way, it appears as though the heavens have decided to listen to us," said Barry. "I'm not sure the angels above have ever heard of just making a phone call."

"Say what you want to say, and the eagle will carry the message up to the heavens for you," said Johnnie. "Then it is up to them if they wish to reply."

"Do I have to say in front of you two?"

Johnnie and Barry looked at each other. Barry shrugged.

"I don't think you need me," he said. "This isn't a vision. It's a direct message."

"Then we will go," said Johnnie, though he didn't look particularly comfortable about the idea. "Just don't say anything to offend them. You have been honored here."

They left, and Diamond was alone on the grass with the eagle in front of her. She didn't feel particularly honored. The bird was looking at her with a blank, almost impatient expression.

She guessed she hadn't expected to get this far. Now that the time had come, she wasn't exactly sure what she wanted to say.

"I'm sorry," she said, eventually. "Sorry about the people who have died for me. I'm sorry about Ty and I'm sorry about

Mrs. Delphine. Wherever they are now, I hope they are being treated well."

She paused to see if the eagle would respond to what she had said; to give her some assurance that they were indeed safe. The eagle did not react at all, so she continued.

"The truth is that I'm afraid. I never wanted to be a leader at any point during my life, but now it looks like people are expecting it. I don't want to make any more choices that lead people to die, but I don't see any way forward that's safe. That's why I need help. That's why you can't ignore us much longer. Without more help on our side, there's a good chance that we'll lose. And then the world will belong to the demons. It'll become... I don't know—a second hell? That doesn't sound good, does it? I'm sure you don't want that."

The eagle blinked at her. It padded the grass impatiently with a claw. Diamond rolled her eyes.

"I guess that's it," she said. "Sorry, I'm boring you."

The eagle took flight with a piercing cry, rising into the sky with a few beats of its wings. It disappeared into the horizon, vanishing into the setting sun.

"Bratty little chicken," Diamond said under her breath, trying to make light of the emotions she was feeling.

In truth, despite the eagle's seeming indifference, she felt better after seeing it disappear into the sky. She had no idea what heaven would make of her message, but it felt like she had shouldered some of the burden she'd been carrying. It felt like she was less alone.

She sat in the grass for a while to ruminate on her thoughts, but a cry from the top of the broadcast tower broke her focus.

"People approaching!" shouted Ida. "They're carrying lights. Everyone in."

Diamond moved at once. She took a deep breath, preparing herself for the possibility of a battle.

*

Diamond gathered on the roof with the others. Ida had her gun loaded and pointed down at the road that broke through the forest, leading right up to the gates of the broadcast tower. On either side of Diamond the half-angels were gathered, wings extended.

They stared down at the road, looking at the beams of flashlights as they neared the compound. By now it was dark—too dark to recognize any faces. The approaching group moved with slow purpose. They didn't seem to be aggressive, but it was impossible to tell.

"Should I fire a warning shot?" Ida asked.

"Maybe," said Diamond. "They can't get in, can they? Let's see if they try the gates."

"Better not to hesitate with matters like this."

But then there was a new kind of light out on the road. Deep white light that pierced darkness: hundreds of sets of wings extended, like beacons in the night.

"They answered," Diamond said, with tears in her eyes. "The half-angels are here!"

CHAPTER ————————9

The gates were opened and the two groups met. Diamond found herself dizzy as she looked around at all of the new faces. In just one night their numbers had swelled from just a couple of dozen to a couple of hundred. There was a complete crowd, and many of them were half-angels.

The heavens were yet to answer her, but the Earth had finally pulled together.

Out of the crowd, a man approached Diamond and shook her hand, introducing himself as Stefan. He looked to be about 40, with olive skin and dark hair. He didn't smile once as Diamond greeted him.

"You don't look as impressive as you did in your broadcast," he said. "You look like a girl. How old are you, seventeen?"

He had a heavy Italian accent to his English. Diamond bristled slightly from the sudden insult. "Old enough to fight and kill demons," she said.

"It is a shame that you could not have prevented a portal from opening at the same time. But no matter. Your broadcast was a good idea." He gestured around him at the gathered crowd. "I came to America as soon as I heard the news that a portal had been opened. In Europe, we have been keeping the forces of hell at bay for hundreds of years. Never before have we let a portal open."

"I'm sorry we haven't lived up to your expectations."

Diamond was starting to get quite sick of speaking to him. She tried to step aside so that she could go and shake hands with someone who didn't make her want to punch them in the face. But Stefan followed alongside her as she walked. He kept his wings extended the whole time, almost like a show of strength.

"I've been gathering a resistance to the hell spawn for weeks," he went on. "You are lucky we were not far from the area when your broadcast was made. As soon as I heard you talking, I saw a chance to grow the strength and numbers of our rebellion."

"*Our* rebellion? You've only just turned up."

"We are fighting for all of us, no? If there are hell spawn walking on this Earth, we fight together."

*

Diamond called a meeting, but there were no rooms in the broadcast tower large enough to accommodate every half-angel. In the end, they went up to the roof, where they filled every part of it. Diamond climbed onto the railing that surrounded the radar dish so that she could be heard over the crowd.

When she surveyed the hundreds of eyes looking at her, Diamond's head began to swim. She couldn't remember ever speaking in front of so many people at once. It had been easier when it was just a camera.

"Thank you for coming," she said. "Until recently, we were led by someone else... but she died trying to take this place. To capture this broadcast tower, we had to take a risk. Our numbers were too small for a real attack. But it looks like that risk has paid off. Now we have numbers, and we don't have to take as many risks anymore. Let's prepare in here and reinforce ourselves. Let's see how many more people we can get to join our cause."

"Not only that," she continued after taking a steadying breath, realizing all of these people were hanging off her every word. "But we have a medicine man among us. We have spoken to heaven and they have listened. If we hold on, then we might be able to get full-blooded angels to join our cause. With heaven's backing, there's no chance that we can lose."

It was what Mrs. Delphine would have planned; Diamond was sure of it. They were strong now, but they could get even stronger.

A polite smattering of applause followed her speech. Diamond found herself blushing but tried to put on a smile. She'd never been great at receiving any kind of praise.

She was just about to tell everyone to go and take it easy for the night when Stefan stood up. Without asking, he walked up to the front of the crowd. He stood atop the same railing as Diamond.

"Thanks to our host," he shouted. "We have a lot of planning to do tomorrow. At ease, soldiers."

Diamond scowled. Signing off her speech was a completely unnecessary show of authority. As the crowd began to disperse, she approached him, jabbing him in the back with a finger.

"For someone who talks a lot about sticking together, you don't mind making me look like an idiot," she said.

"I didn't agree with your plan," said Stefan. "Those who have been following me are going to fight. As intended."

"Like I said, I've spoken to the heavens."

"You might have *thought* you did, but the heavens don't just speak to random mortals. In Europe, our ancient order of defenders has prayed for centuries, and not once has a full angel appeared to us."

"Right. You couldn't do it, so we can't either?"

"I don't want to argue with you," he said, though every bit of his tone suggested that arguing was something he reveled in. "But just so we're clear: I intend to fight as soon as possible. I thought that broadcast of yours was a rallying cry." He shook his head. "Sounds like this is going to have been a waste of time."

He walked off. Diamond stared daggers into the back of his head.

Of course that was her luck. She sent out a message to ask anyone in the world for help, and the person who responded was the most pig-headed idiot in the Northern Hemisphere.

Even more ironically, she'd been the one fighting for the rash decision up until now. The one time she wanted to be cautious and think of a new strategy, she had a new risk taker to deal with.

*

Over the coming days, as more and more half-angels arrived at the broadcast tower, it was apparent that two camps were forming.

Outside of the tower, Stefan and many of the others had thrown together shelters. Every day, there seemed to be more, until the surrounding field looked like a campsite at Coachella. They had even built targets out of plywood and had mounted them on the wire fence, which they used for rifle practice.

Those outside stopped entering the tower for the regular meetings that Diamond was holding to keep her own followers' morale high. Whenever Diamond looked out from the roof of the broadcast tower, she could see Stefan wandering from shelter to shelter, bringing in his "bros" into big man hugs. Occasionally, he would stop someone at target practice and take their rifle out of their hands, demonstrating how they weren't quite holding it properly, giving some condescending speech about the need to be prepared.

They *did* look prepared. Her loyal half-angels looked confused and lost by comparison.

"Do you think he might be right?" Diamond asked Lucas one night.

Lucas had managed to recover somewhat from Mrs. Delphine's death by then. He still couldn't say her name without crying, but at least he could hold conversations and smile when he needed to now. "He's not right at all," said Lucas. "We've been waiting for a retaliation ever since you sent out that broadcast. But where is it? I think they know we've got a good spot here. They don't want to face us outright. Stefan wants to march right out into their city. He'd be walking those people right out of safety and into the laps of the enemy."

"Right," said Diamond. "But he's going to do that no matter what we say. And when he does, we'll have lost our advantage."

"He's screwed us either way, then."

Diamond stared out over the horizon, over to where the city slept. It looked as though the city's power was getting patchy. Every night it seemed that dozens more lights had gone out, and now the city was plunged into near darkness.

At least they won't be able to see either, now, she thought. Then she paused and pursed her lips.

That was right. They were probably searching the streets with flashlights now. When she had been there, the place was already a hotbed of pickpockets and attackers. With the near-total dark, she bet that anyone could move about in their private business, and the LGs would have a nightmare trying to track them down.

"Lucas," she said. "I've got an idea. Get Ida, Marco, Sepharius Jerome, and Johnnie." She paused. "Barry as well. We might need to take matters into our own hands."

*

They gathered in the director's office, which was just about the only room in the whole building that had a lock and offered privacy.

If they weren't facing the potential apocalypse, Diamond might have managed to laugh as she looked at her friends seated around the table. With one angel, a seer, a half-angel, a misty-eyed kid, an agent in a bulletproof vest, and a sick man in bandages thrown in for good measure, they looked like the weirdest boardroom ever.

"We're running out of time," she said. "If Stefan decides he's going to attack the city head-on, then we blow our shot. We won't get another fighting force like this one. It'll be a massacre."

"He means to attack in a day," said Sepharius, grimly. "I heard it from someone else who had been down there to listen to him. A lot of the other ex-prisoners are heading down there now, Diamond."

"Stefan is attacking, and we can't change that. But what we can do is try to bring the odds in our favor as quickly as possible."

"I'm not sure I like where this is going," said Ida.

"Lucas. Marco. Johnnie. Do any of you know if it's possible to close a portal to hell?"

Lucas and Marco exchanged concerned looks. Johnnie, predictably, was staring off into space.

"Theoretically," said Lucas. "But that portal will have been growing from the day it opened, which was months ago now, Diamond. There will be demons and Vipers pouring from it every day."

"If it can be closed, there's a chance."

"It would take a lot of divine energy," said Lucas. "I've read about it in one of Mrs. Delphine's books. Arch-angels used to close portals to hell. I've never heard of a mortal doing it."

"Don't look at me," said Barry.

"I wasn't."

"Whatever the theory," said Diamond. "We have to try. And we have to move quickly. If we can close the portal at the same time that Stefan leads his attack, then we can prevent hell from calling in reinforcements. We can give the forces of Earth the best chance of success. Otherwise, what hope is there?"

The group fell into silence. It was a gruesome plan, which would involve at least some of them entering parts of the city that were completely dominated by demons and their servants.

Diamond shuddered at the thought of the demons, and half-demons, that she'd fought in the past. The idea of facing more than one at once—an entire *army* of them, in fact—filled her with dread.

"I believe in Diamond's plan," said Johnnie. "The more that we try, the more that heaven will know the determination and conviction in our hearts. We must counteract the corruption and selfishness of the world."

"I have no idea what Johnnie just said," said Lucas. "But you can count me in as well."

"And me," said Ida.

"You can always count on me, Diamond," said Marco.

Diamond shook her head, smiling at him sadly. "You know you're too unwell to help with this. You need to stay somewhere safe, with Johnnie."

"Not a chance. We're not breaking up again, Diamond. We need to stick together."

"I agree," said Johnnie. "All of our paths head to the same point now. Apart, we can be picked off. Together, we present a united front. Both to our allies and our enemies."

"I can keep an eye on the wounded," said Jerome. "We can get close to the city but keep to the tree line. If we need to, I can help people hide."

Diamond wasn't happy, but Marco's face was determined, and she knew that she wouldn't be able to argue with him.

Besides, they were entering the end game. Diamond looked at the determined faces of each one of her friends and felt absolute gratitude in her heart that they were here; that they trusted her.

Only Sepharius looked unsure.

"I haven't known you very long," she said. "But everything you've just described sounds risky. I need to be with my half-angels. If all of us come, then this won't be a covert mission, will it? You'll all be seen, and this will all have been for nothing."

Diamond forgave her at once, even though it stung. She understood that Sepharius had her loyalties. That meant Diamond was going to be the only half-angel out there trying to close the portal. If any demons or Vipers showed up, the bulk of the fighting would be up to her.

Despite that fact, the plan was set in motion. They would leave the next evening just as the sun was setting, moving in darkness so that no LGs would be able to see them coming. Stefan would be leading the fight to capture the city. Diamond would be leading the charge to save it.

When the meeting was over, everyone stood up to leave. One by one they filed out of the room. Diamond embraced every single person warmly. As far as she knew, these were the last few moments she might ever have with some of them.

Only Barry remained seated at the desk. Diamond guessed he was sulking, and turned to leave him there in the office, but he cleared his throat. She turned to face him.

"Let's talk," he said.

"About what, Barry? If this is about anything other than you helping us, then I don't have the time to waste on it."

"Sit. For heaven's sake—I'm your father and we haven't said a civil word to each other in weeks."

"Don't use the 'f-word' around me."

"Just sit."

He sounded earnest. Emotional, even. Diamond had never heard him sound anything close to that before. She sat down at the desk again and he looked her in the eyes, his brow crumpled and serious.

"I'll help," he said. "But not for heaven. Not for the Earth. I'll help because you're my daughter, and I don't want to see you get killed."

"That's nice," said Diamond. "Look at you being all dad-like."

"I'm serious. I have no trust in heaven, but I've got trust in you, Diamond. If you'll let me come, I'll help you close this portal."

Diamond felt a tear sting the corner of her eye, which she rubbed away. She pushed the emotion down into the pit of her stomach, where she buried all of the complex emotions that she held about her parents.

She never, not once in her life, ever felt as though she could trust them. That lack of trust had killed any expectation that she had about them being helpful.

But here was her father, offering to risk his life for her. It didn't nearly make up for the years of strain between them, but it was something. She and her dad were not too different from each other. They were both pigheaded, strong-willed, and full of attitude.

"I still get to keep the sword, right?" Diamond said.

Barry grinned.

CHAPTER ――――――10

The gates to the compound were opened at dawn. Diamond went down to see their short-lived allies leave. Not that anyone took notice of her. They were listening to Stefan, who stood at the threshold of the gates, addressing the half-angels that followed him. Unlike Diamond, there were no nerves at all in his voice when he talked to his people. This was a guy who knew how to lead, and Diamond felt childish with how jealous she felt.

"We will reach the city by noon," he said. "When I give the order, spread your wings and fight for your lives. We have to put a stop to this hellish mess before it consumes everything!"

The half-angels cheered. When Stefan finished talking, they began to march. As quickly as she could, Diamond took Stefan aside.

"One last time: Please—can't you wait?" she asked him. "Another couple of days. Anything."

"There is no waiting now," said Stefan, turning. "Goodbye, Diamond."

"You're a pigheaded idiot, you know that, right?"

"And you. Maybe in some other circumstances, we might have got on a little better."

Diamond watched them leave. As the last of the crowd peeled through the gates, she realized that they were back down to next to nothing. Just her, her friends, and a dozen or so people from the reserve.

Jerome brought packs for them with a few basic supplies inside. It took a while for them to figure out the mechanics of the next few steps. Many of them said they planned to return to the reserve. Diamond had Lucas, Marco, Barry, Ida, Johnnie, and Jerome with her. She winced watching them prepare to leave. It took Marco almost five minutes just to muster the energy to stand.

"Let's go, then," said Diamond. "For humanity, I guess."

*

They followed the path that Stefan and his half-angels had taken. It was marked by discarded cans, food wrappers, and footprints in the dirt at the side of the road.

"They're making a good pace," said Lucas. "You think we'll catch up with them?"

"Probably," said Ida. "We should slip by them. When people are riled up for fighting it isn't a good idea to surprise them."

"Didn't you used to be a preacher?"

"I trained with the LG," she said. "A lot of the leaders there are ex-military."

"Of course. Great."

Diamond wasn't completely listening to what they were saying. She was focusing on the city as they got near to it, trying to get a handle on how far they were from civilization. They walked over the face of a huge two-lane road, which was completely abandoned. She looked left, then right, and there wasn't a single flicker of light to be seen.

As they kept walking, however, she saw lights far ahead of them. They didn't look to be electric, but the flicker of flames.

Then she heard the gunfire.

Ida froze at once and beckoned them off the road. There wasn't anything to be seen, but coming from about five hundred meters in front of them there were the sounds of a fray. People were screaming in pain, and there were other noises. Noises that made Diamond shudder; that reminded her of an encounter she'd had not long before.

A dark, sinister chuckle was followed by mad, wild roaring: The sounds of a demon, hungry for blood. A man's scream rang out through the night, suddenly cut off.

"It's Stefan and those other half-angels," said Barry. "They've walked right into an attack."

"We should help them," said Diamond, at once.

"And get ourselves killed? Don't forget that we've come here to sneak in and try and end this. We've barely walked for an hour and you want us to throw ourselves to the demons already?"

"He's right," said Ida. "If we attack we won't be helping anyone. We'll lose our advantage."

"That's what we do now, is it?" said Lucas. "We just abandon people in need?"

The three of them looked to Diamond for direction. Diamond felt the weight of their trust in her. She couldn't say that she fully understood why they believed in her, but Mrs. Delphine wouldn't have questioned it. She would have led her people into whatever she thought was right.

"We're going to approach carefully," said Diamond. "Keep under cover. If we can help as we approach, we help."

Barry groaned and Ida bit her lip, but neither of them argued. Diamond led them into the bushes that lined the side of the road and forged a careful path through the undergrowth.

*

They neared the site of the battle and saw that it was over. Flames licked the trees around them, burning them down to withered, blackened branches. There were bodies on the ground: humans, half-angels, Vipers, and one demon.

The demon was larger than the one Diamond and Marco had fought. Its body was struck with a thousand cuts and nicks, and it bled out black onto the ground. Stefan stood at the center of the gathering, trying to calm people down.

About half of the people who had left with him were still on their feet. By the white light of their flashlight beams, Diamond could see wide eyes and pale faces. It was a far cry from the confident, enraptured battle party that had left the broadcast tower.

"I don't want to hear anything," said Stefan, catching sight of Diamond as she approached the gathering. "This isn't a time for 'I told you so's.'"

"We didn't come to gloat. We came to help," said Diamond.

"Well, you're a bit late for that aren't you?"

Ida scowled and looked about ready to kick Stefan's ass. She made a step towards him, but Diamond blocked her path with an outstretched arm. "You're right," said Diamond. "We are."

"It doesn't matter. We're moving on to the city!"

He shouted in the same rousing voice he had used back at the broadcast tower, but this time his shouting was met with silence. Everyone stared at Stefan like they couldn't believe what they had heard, his followers included.

"You can't be serious. You've lost half of you already against just *one* demon and its Vipers. What hope do you think you have if you attack now?"

"The only hope," said Stefan. "It's this or losing."

"This *is* losing." Diamond gestured all around herself at the bodies littering the floor. Stefan took in the scene and his expression changed. His determination was replaced with fear, as though he were truly seeing the carnage of the battle for the first time. He opened his mouth and then closed it again.

Diamond put a hand on his shoulder, and he didn't cringe away. "I know you're going to fight," she said. "I know I can't stop you. But we're going to try and close the portal. We're going to sneak into the place where it was opened and stop this demon invasion from growing any larger."

"That won't work. You try and close that portal and you'll attract the retribution of Lucifer himself."

Lucifer. Diamond grimaced. The devil himself. She was taking on the *devil*.

But she supposed they had been taking on the devil ever since they decided to fight. This was no different. If Diamond was going to meet the mastermind behind all this violence, then so be it. Better to face one fallen angel than an entire army of demons.

"You take your path, and I'll take mine," she said.

"I'll remember that when I'm fighting. I don't expect I'll see you again." He smiled at her. The first smile that Diamond had ever seen on the man's hard face. "I don't agree with a single word that comes out of your mouth, Diamond. But I do respect you for trying to undo the mess that has been made here."

Diamond smiled back at him, even though the comment was still sort of an insult. In the short time that she had gotten to know the man, she realized she was unlikely to get anything better out of him.

CHAPTER ————————11

Diamond decided that they should stay with Lucas and the others as they neared the city, to be ready to support them if more fighting should break out. No one seemed to agree with her approach, but Diamond was determined.

She couldn't help it: Every time she looked at Stefan, she saw a proud, determined man. His approach wasn't the right one, but he was still going ahead with it. She couldn't just watch him and the others die without knowing that he tried to support them.

They kept to the banks of the Mississippi and the trees thinned out as they entered parkland. The place was near pitch black. Most of the streetlights were no longer being powered, casting an eerie darkness over the city.

If demons slithering around wasn't bad enough, the green spaces were deserted. Ahead of them, the high rises of the inner city rose in great shadows, like silent tombstones in a crypt.

Stefan ordered them to stop and spent a long time watching the city. Occasional beams from flashlights swept the far end of the park, spending a lot of time peering around every corner. They were waiting, keeping a watch.

"Let's hold here and get ready," said Stefan. "Any further and we'll be in their search perimeter. We need to prepare for anything. I'm going to think about tactics. We'll be ready to fight in a matter of a few hours."

The gathering of half-angels nodded. They were shaken, but Stefan was still the one leader that they had.

A few hours, thought Diamond as she looked at the city again. It looked peaceful now, but she knew that it was sleeping; biding its moment. They were staring at a hornet's nest. As soon as they struck it, it would open with all the fury that the hells could offer.

These people were going to die, Diamond knew. They wouldn't last longer than an hour. But there was nothing she could do; Stefan wasn't going to listen to her.

She sat down in the grass. It was wet from rain, and the cold soaked through her jeans. Diamond didn't care. She looked up at the stars with desperation.

Ida, Barry, and Lucas sat down around her. Barry put an arm around her shoulder, and for once, Diamond didn't shy away. She needed comfort from someone. Even him.

"Can we ask for help one more time?" said Diamond.

"You've already spoken to the heavens once. Believe me, they didn't listen to you then, they won't listen now," said Barry.

"Not for us? For them?" She gestured over to where Stefan and the others were gathered, loading firearms, and comparing blades. "They need protection. If the heavens care at all, they won't let this become a massacre."

"You're still giving them far too much credit."

"Pray with me. It will mean more, coming from an angel."

She met Barry's eyes. He was scowling, but he didn't say "no." He groaned like a child being asked to do something they didn't want to do, but then he clasped his hands together.

"Fine," he said. "But let's just do this the old-fashioned way. I haven't got time for any fancy rituals. It's been a while since I've spoken to anyone up there," he said. "You'll know I'm not doing this for you, but for my daughter. But that doesn't lessen the need behind this prayer. People are going to die. I know that is just another business day for all of you, but this battle could be the beginning of the end. We've tried to fight on our own, and we're going to keep trying. You know the odds are against us. These people need help. Protect them. Watch over them. At least give them some respect and attention, for the love of all the heavens."

He unclasped his hands. For a while, all four of them watched the sky. It began to drizzle. Raindrops trickled gently down their faces, but they still kept watching.

Diamond was beginning to lose hope. It was beginning to feel stupid, talking into a void.

But then there was light. The unmistakable arched shape of wings. A figure soared down towards them in a spiral, and he was bearing a sword; a sword just like Diamond's. It glowed with a divine light.

Barry looked stunned. "They've sent Michael."

"As in, Archangel Michael?" Diamond asked, a rising excitement in her chest.

"I'm going to kill him."

*

Archangels, it turned out, did not look precisely like other angels. At least, Michael did not look anything like her father. He stood at seven feet. His eyes were deep blue, proud, and youthful. His face was angular. His jaw was heavy set, and the ridges of his features were sharp as knives.

Looking at his face, it was hard to place his age. He had the determination, pride, and self-confidence of a much older man, but in the right light, he only looked 20. Around his body was clad a royal blue robe that illuminated a soft, calming glow. On either side of him, his silver-glistened wings were outstretched. They were almost double the span of Diamond's.

"Greetings, Diamond," he said. "Daughter of heaven, your words have been heard and considered. Your hope was great, and your faith has been tested. I come to you now among the gathering darkness to tell you that humanity is not alone. Now as in ancient times, the heavens will protect the Earth. The ancient covenant between Creator and creation will be renewed."

"You still don't know how to talk normally, do you?" said Barry.

Michael turned to face him, disgust and judgment on his face. "Good evening, Barry," he said. "It was pleasant to hear from you again."

Barry didn't hesitate. He swung his fist and struck Michael in the face.

Michael barely reacted. His head bent back just a few centimeters, but when Barry pulled his fist away, there wasn't a single mark upon it.

"You're as charming as ever," said Michael.

"You're just going to stand there. After everything you've done to me. After you and those other high-minded idiots just ignored me?"

"We heard your prayers. How could we have intervened? We are bound not to present ourselves on Earth except in times of great need."

"I think being tortured counts in my book as great need."

"Your need. Not the need of the many."

"You are arrogant, aren't you?"

Michael didn't respond to that. His face was completely indifferent. He took the criticism of his actions with absolute acceptance, and he didn't seek to justify himself one bit. Diamond thought that Barry had a point. Who exactly was this ally that had been sent to her?

"Why now?" she said. "You saw countless people die and you didn't do anything."

"The lot of being divine is knowing when to act, and when to ignore. There is nothing more important to us than the free will of people. They suffer greatly, but they choose how they respond to crisis. Until now, humanity had chosen darkness. Many have served Lucifer, and we cannot pretend otherwise."

"They were frightened. And hopeless."

"There was a time when faith was a given. Faith today does not exist."

"Perhaps it would if you helped out more often."

"I did not come here to argue with mortals. I came here to fight for the selfless."

As he spoke, his sword came alive with flames. Now that he was closer to them, Diamond could see that Michael's sword was longer than her own. The blade reached five feet and was nearly a foot in breadth. Anyone else would have held it with two hands. Michael held it aloft with a single arm, as though it weighed nothing at all.

"If all of you gathered here are willing to fight for your freedom, then I will do what I can," Michael said, his voice echoing over the parks with the strength of thunder. It was loud enough that Diamond was sure that those in the city would have been able to hear it, too. Stefan and the others had gathered to watch, spellbound by the arrival of this new, great ally. "Many of you gathered here hold the blood of the divine. You have angelic power that is linked to the heavens, and that is weakened when you are apart from them. Let me awaken in you now your full potential. Let your human side dim, and your angelic energy shine forth!"

As he spoke, Diamond felt a rush of adrenaline through her body. A warm feeling in her stomach was spreading outwards, running through her veins. Without willing them, her wings unfurled. They were glowing, just as Michael's were glowing. She felt every emotion she had held over the last few days escalate. All of her hope. Her strength. Her fear. Her sorrow. Her guilt. It reached a fever pitch, and she could *see* it emanating from her body.

As she looked across the crowds gathered, she could see all of their emotions, as well. They rippled out from their bodies, filling the air with strange, curling light. When she looked at their emotional auras, she could feel their feelings in her heart.

As she glanced at Stefan, she could feel his anger... as well as his fear, which he was trying so hard to repress.

When she looked at Lucas, she saw the hope and the wonder at what he was witnessing.

Then she looked at Marco. She could sense his strength renewing as he stood, no longer weakened. The curse from the demon's blade was still there, however; a stain on an otherwise pure and joyful presence.

She approached him and rested her hands upon his wounded shoulder. She found she could peel away the curse as easily as a Band-Aid. As she touched it with her fingers, black smoke left his body, rising into the sky.

"Every one of you has heavenly power that will be guided by your human spirit," Michael continued. "For you, Diamond, your empathy makes you sensitive to others. Now you can sense and repair their souls. Marco, your power comes from your courage, and your willingness to fight for others. Your strength and speed have become heroic, and you will be able to fight in the name of others for as long as you wish."

Marco's eyes were wide with wonder. He spread his newly sprouted wings and shot high into the air. He moved at a speed that caused an updraft of wind that almost toppled Diamond to the ground. He whooped with glee as he rocketed high above them, unbound and free.

Barry was still the same as before. To Diamond, he looked even more desperate and drained now, compared to her heavenly gift. Even though he was a full-blooded angel, it was as though his divinity had nearly abandoned him completely. She could sense just barely a whisper of power in him.

Michael turned to him. "I can help you too, Barry," he said. "But only if you're willing to let go of the past."

Barry scoffed. "That's easy to say," he said. "You haven't lived my past."

"The future is more important. Think of the life you can have with your daughter, as soon as all of you are free."

Barry looked at Diamond. He met her eyes with intensity.

For once, Diamond didn't have an urge to look away. She was feeling better than she had ever felt, and she wanted her father to share in it.

"Fine," he said. "For the future."

Michael rested a hand upon his head, and Barry's wings unfurled. He rose to his feet, growing taller and stronger. His eyes came alive with a new life. His beard thickened and grew.

He didn't look like a wreck anymore. Standing tall and proud, his whole being glowing with divine energy. He looked like a proud Viking warrior. He grinned.

"That *does* feel good," he said. "Like old times."

"You look respectable," said Michael. Then he turned to the crowd. "Come forth, children of heaven. Today, we fight together!"

A chorus of cheers. Diamond joined them.

For the first time, it was beginning to look as though they might have a chance.

CHAPTER ——————12

"I agree that you should not fight," Michael said once Diamond had told him their plan.

"You think a portal can be closed?"

"It can be. You will face great resistance, though."

"Lucifer?"

"Possibly. But our once great brother's arrogance and pride outweigh his strength. Caught unaware, you may be able to match him. Especially with the help of your friends."

Diamond nodded, though it wasn't exactly the certainty she had been hoping for when she'd begun speaking to him.

Around her, the great attack on Minneapolis was beginning to take shape. Half-angels, looking grander than ever, were standing proud. Archangel Michael summoned a holy sword for each of them, and the sight of them in rows in the night was majestic. A crowd of heavenly beacons, all wielded with purpose and strength.

But the city was beginning to move, as well. There were shapes in the darkness, just at the edges of the urban center of the city. Hordes of Vipers were there and, behind them, much larger figures.

"Are we ready?" Stefan roared. His voice carried like thunder now, just as Michael's had.

A group of half-angels, their spirit renewed, roared back at him. As if in answer, the demons in the city roared, as well. Theirs was a cry of anger and fury rather than triumph.

The night darkened, and Archangel Michael led the charge.

The half-angels flew across the grass in a dance of lights. Vipers ran out to meet them. Swords cut through flesh. From such a distance, Diamond couldn't see the full battle, but she didn't see the light of any of the heavenly swords go out.

They were crushing the demons that were waiting for them. None of them had expected an archangel to appear. Finally, Diamond had the element of surprise.

"Come on," Ida said in her ear. "We need to get away from here if we're going to keep ourselves hidden."

Diamond nodded, though she couldn't look away from the battle. It was going well now, but when the demons began fighting, they would start to count losses.

"It doesn't feel right to me, either, but we have a job to do. We have to do it, for them. For everyone."

"I know," said Diamond. "Let's go."

*

Diamond and Ida wandered out over the hilltops, leaving Johnnie and Jerome behind. They were going to camp in the woods, to keep as safe as possible. Diamond hadn't been expecting to have Marco fighting by her side, but turning to see him looking stronger than ever bolstered her confidence.

"It's a long way to Abe's mansion," he said.

"We're going to need to camp tonight," said Diamond.

He nodded.

"Maybe we can talk? In private?"

Lucas chuckled, clearly eavesdropping. "Please find somewhere private. Believe me, none of us want to see or hear whatever you hormone-riddled teenagers get up to."

Diamond rolled her eyes at him but grinned. It felt good to still be laughing. Just a short while before, she wasn't sure if she would ever laugh again.

*

They reached a hill overlooking Abe's home at around midnight. They were too far away from the battle now to see how it was going, so Diamond just had to hope it was being fought well. Abe's mansion stood alone, away from the bustle of the city. It was alive with activity, though. Flashlights swept the place, and Diamond didn't have to be any closer to know that demons were waiting. She could feel their boredom, having been left on guard duty. She could feel their hunger, as well.

As the others made a quick camp at the top of the hill, she walked with Marco down into the tree line, where they could be in private. No one stopped them, or even said a word when they saw them leaving. Her friends knew how important it was that they had this time together.

They sat on the banks of the Mississippi, staring at a huge full moon that was reflected on the surface of the water. The air was still and calm, broken only by the gentle buzzing of insects.

"It's crazy how we can still find places as peaceful as this," Diamond said. "Even in the middle of all this madness."

"You still don't want to talk about us?"

"I don't need to talk." Diamond smiled at him. "I can feel your nerves. I know your palms are starting to sweat, and you're worried about saying the wrong thing."

"I guess I don't need to tell you how I'm feeling anymore. Can you sense anything else?"

"A lot of love."

Marco was too much of a nervous mess. He sure as hell wasn't going to do it, so Diamond leaned forward, meeting his lips with hers. It was a slow, romantic kiss at first, but it became more and more passionate. Diamond ran her fingers through his hair. He held her close enough that she could hardly breathe, but she didn't care.

Embracing like that, while she could sense everything that he was feeling, was another level of intimacy. Every brush of tongue made her gasp. Every movement of his body against hers made her dizzy.

It felt as though they kissed forever, but when they broke apart, the night was as broad and dark as ever. They looked for a while into each other's eyes. Diamond allowed herself to get lost in the well of shared emotion that was deepening between them.

"What are we going to do when this is all over?" she said.

"Be together. We can stay like this, forever."

"Or we might die."

Marco laughed. "I've never met someone who is an optimist and a pessimist at the same time," he said.

"I'm a realist." She chuckled and turned around where she was sitting so that she could look up at the stars. "You know this might never be over. You and Mrs. Delphine had been fighting Vipers forever before all of this started. They're still going to be around, even if we close this portal and win the fight for the city."

"Then we'd better be thankful for each peaceful night that we get. This one included."

They put together the tent that Jerome had lent them. They worked without saying another word, pausing just now and then to share a smile or a knowing glance. When it was done they lay down in it together.

Diamond couldn't imagine an intimate moment being more perfect. She was in tune with his every emotion. It was as though Marco could read her emotions, as well, and Diamond trusted him with them completely. It wasn't often she allowed herself to be vulnerable. All of her life she had put up emotional walls to protect herself, and to make other people see her as strong.

In the tent with Marco, she forgot about the pressure on their shoulders and the task that she had to complete. For one night, it was just the two of them. He stroked her hair, and Diamond nuzzled into his neck. They kissed and talked about the future. A future where they could be a normal couple, going to the movies, cuddling on a couch somewhere. It was a future that might not even exist, if things went wrong. But it still felt good to pretend.

When they awoke together, no words needed to be exchanged. They both knew that they had formed a physical and emotional bond that would last a lifetime.

CHAPTER ————————13

When they rejoined the others at dawn, no one commented on their absence. The only recognition at all was a knowing smirk from Lucas, which Diamond thumped him on the shoulder for.

Barry looked out over the mansion. Since Michael had awoken him, it was like he had been reborn as a new man. He stood as tall and proud as he had when his divine spirit had been awoken the first time.

"We should move soon," he said. "Many of the Vipers and LGs guarding the place have started to move out. I think their attention is being directed elsewhere."

At once, Diamond was brought back to reality. "The battle?"

Barry nodded grimly. "If they're still fighting. It seems as though the full force of hell is being directed against them."

Diamond looked down at her feet. All of her guilt was renewed. Part of her still believed she should be back there, helping them. Ida seemed to be able to sense how she was feeling.

"We made the right choice," she said. "If the LGs and Vipers are being called to fight, then it must be because they're struggling to get the upper hand. This is a good thing."

"I hope you're right."

"Let's move."

*

They stuck to the tree line in the grounds of Abe's manor, keeping themselves in the shade. It was better to approach by night. No flashlight beams were running across the grounds, and no one seemed to be on the lookout. They reached the edge of the grounds and ducked behind a Gothic tower, low to the gravel.

Lucas focused, his eyes going pale for a moment. "I can see two auras in the guts of that place," he said. "Too strong to be human. Stronger even than the demon that was guarding us in the tower. I think they might be arch-demons. Dark ones."

"Dark ones?" Diamond asked.

"Lucifer's answer to the greatest warriors in the heavens. Ex-angels twisted and shaped beyond comprehension into huge and powerful monsters. Two of them. This isn't going to be easy."

"Nothing's easy anymore," said Barry. "But let's strike now before they can get any assistance."

"Someone's coming," said Lucas.

"Let them come," said Diamond, unfurling her wings.

Two armed LGs came around the corner a few moments later. For a few seconds, they froze, shocked at the intruders. Then one lifted the barrel of his gun and squeezed the trigger.

Barry charged in front of them, bending his wings around to cover the front of his body. The gunfire bounced off of his wings as though the bullets were made of rubber.

As soon as Barry opened his wings, Marco sped ahead, his sword blazing. He cut down the two guards before they even had time to shout.

Barry led, and Marco and Diamond followed. More LGs followed the first two, but not as many as there should have been. Five guards unleashed automatic fire at the divine warriors, but bullets weren't going to hurt them anymore.

Diamond could feel the fear of their enemies as she launched high into the air with a single mighty flap of her wings. Then she descended, her boot heel connecting directly with a soldier's face.

She felt the guard's neck snap and his body went limp. The others screamed and moved to retaliate, but she was already slashing with her sword, blinding them with the divine light of the blade. Then Marco and Barry were on either side of her, slashing in unison.

In the space of 10 seconds, there were no more guards outside the building. The place was completely clear. They stood, not even having broken a sweat.

"The demons know we're here," said Lucas. "They're preparing themselves around the portal."

"You and Ida wait here," said Diamond. "Keep a watch for any more LGs, and take them out. If anything worse shows up, I'll know; I'll feel your panic."

"I don't panic, kid, but Lucas might," said Ida. She took a post over a wall surrounding the inner garden, her eyes already scanning for enemies. There was a shout from the far end of the grounds and she let forth a burst of gunfire. The shouting was gone. "We've got you covered. Get inside!"

*

They entered through the front door, which Diamond found very strange. The last time she had been there it was as a guest. Now she was storming the place with a sword ablaze.

She knew the way to go. Every step through the twisted halls of that place brought back horrible, guilty memories. She had been there when this had all started, and she'd been unable to stop it.

We're going to stop it now, she promised herself. *That all doesn't matter anymore. What matters is what we do next.*

As they took the stairs down to the basement, the heat became suddenly, unbearably intense. Sweat ran down Diamond's back as she led the march toward the basement, determined not to let her fear slow her progress. She could sense her friends' fear as well, and she didn't want to do anything to break their courage. She had to stay strong, for all of them.

Down either side of the walls were deep gouges. Claw marks from demons that had been summoned and had scraped their way to the world above. Diamond tried not to look at them.

The further down they went, the more there was an overbearing smell in the air. It smelt like sulfur; like smoke, char, and heat. It made her want to gag, but Diamond resisted the urge as she kept on marching.

The door to the basement was burst into splinters. There was no barrier between her and the great shadows waiting on the inside. Diamond drew her sword.

"You were brave to come back, child," one of the Dark Ones said. Its voice was barely more than a whisper, but it carried through the room and seemed to come from all directions at once. "Foolish, but brave."

The skeletal creatures stepped out from the shadows. They were enormous, filling the basement as they stood side by side.

Their bodies were hunched, with cracked bones that burst out of fetid, open flesh. Their eyes were fire, and in their hands were great axes, with heads that were alive with ethereal, unnatural fire.

"The archangel has sent you here to die in its place," said the other Dark One. This one laughed as he talked, as though every bit of their pain and fear were a joke to it. "We knew they were cowardly, but this is pathetic."

"Take one step closer and I'll cut you down," said Diamond.

"You feel our emotions, child. You think we have any fear of you?"

Diamond gritted her teeth. They didn't hold any fear at all. All she sensed from them was a morbid determination. To the Dark Ones, Diamond, Marco, and Barry were just pests to be crushed.

But these pests had fought demons before.

Marco moved first, moving at speed from the stairwell straight into the space between the two Dark Ones. His sword was a lightning bolt as it cut through the air, piercing darkness.

A Dark One swung an axe at him. It missed, striking air, but it sent out a shock wave of rippling flames that scorched Marco's body, sending him spinning to the ground. He was on his feet in moments, but his skin was blistered and bruised.

Diamond moved alongside her dad. Barry blocked an axe swing with his sword, seemingly unaffected by the flames that struck him. Diamond struck the Dark One that attacked her father, sending her sword into its chattering skull.

Splinters of bone burst from the Dark One's face. As Diamond landed, she raised an arm to cover her face from the white shards. They cut her skin open, spraying blood and stinging enough to make her cry out. When she lowered her arm, the Dark One she had struck was still standing.

Its face had a great cut down the middle and its bone was ripped apart like a split log; but its wild jaw was still chattering with laughter. The next axe swing was aimed at her. Diamond flew to one side, only to collide with the other Dark One, which gripped her throat with a large, bony hand, lifting her from the ground.

The Dark One lifted her until she was at a level with its face. Its breath was like a butcher's counter. The pressure on her neck was unbelievable; so strong that she was sure her neck would snap any moment.

Marco saved her, cutting the Dark One's hand at the wrist. It screamed—the first sign that these monsters could feel pain—and Diamond collapsed to the ground in a heap. She felt arms under her, and when she was back on her feet, she was on the other side of the room at the stairwell, Marco and Barry on either side of her. The injured Dark One was still clutching at its severed limb. The other was moving towards them, fury in its eyes. It was no longer laughing.

"We have no chance if we attack on our own," said Barry. "We have to coordinate this and fight together. Marco can move fastest. Keep them distracted, and I'll strike them where they're weakest. Diamond, you be ready to attack right after me."

Diamond nodded. They didn't need to discuss it any further.

Marco charged, exactly as Barry had said. He soared over the top of both of their heads and struck downwards with his sword, peppering both from above with thrusts and stabs.

As they turned their attention upwards, Barry moved. With mighty strength he swung his sword in an arch, severing a Dark One at the ankles.

The demon collapsed to the ground, just as Diamond joined the fray. She swung down her sword in a killing blow; a cleaving arc that wrenched the Dark One's head from its shoulders. The monster roared and writhed, but it was bested. The flames on its axe went out as it slowly went still.

The other Dark One stared as Marco landed. Now it was facing three sword-wielding divine soldiers. Diamond could sense fear at last.

"I thought you weren't frightened," she said. "I didn't realize that demons were scared of mortals."

"You know nothing of fear, child. But you will."

It stepped backward towards the portal, resting a hand on the black stone ring that outlined it. The Dark One began to speak in a strange language—a guttural garble that was foul to hear.

"Kill it," said Barry. "Now. Or everything we've fought for won't be worth it."

Diamond charged, but it was too late. The portal exploded with flames, sending them all flying backward, crashing into the basement wall. The room was filled with smoke. The paintings and wallpaper began to crisp and burn. There was a figure in the flames: The outline of a man covered with curling shadow.

Diamond tried to sense the emotions of the new arrival, but there was nothing there; just a cold, dead heart. She charged, trying to end the call of Lucifer before it had a chance to come to fruition. But whenever she moved forward, flames forced her back. They dragged at her body and licked at her skin.

Diamond retreated with the others to the stairwell.

The flames died down. As the sounds of their roaring fury quenched, there was a new noise. The sound of slow applause.

The figure that stepped out of the inferno was a man. His skin was pale. His hair was blond, curled, and cut to a stylish cut.

The devil was handsome. Every single feature on his face dripped with seduction.

"Miss Diamond," said Lucifer. "I've been watching you for some time, my dear. And I have to say, I'm rather interested."

CHAPTER ———————14

Stefan beat his wings and thundered past a barrage of gunfire. With a glance downwards, he saw the gathering of LGs on the roof of a huge skyscraper. He opened his palm, and from it launched a burst of holy fire down towards the roof of the building where it burst like a firework.

When he looked again, most of the guards were on the floor, not moving.

"Concentrate on the demons," said Archangel Michael. "They are the true strength in this fight."

"I know what I'm doing," Stefan said.

"If we don't fight in unity, we don't stand a chance."

Stefan gritted his teeth and then nodded. He turned his attention to the skies around him.

Demons were flying on grotesque, bat-like wings. They were great hulking brutes who could move across the sky quicker than Stefan could keep track of with his eyes. Their strength was terrifying. Stefan had already watched them grab half-angels out of the sky, flinging them down towards the ground as though they were insects.

While they were wild and barbaric in their fighting, they lacked any kind of coordination. That had to be their weakness.

"With me!" Stefan screamed as he soared past three of his half-angels. With their swords flashing, they flew directly towards the nearest demon. It turned over in the sky, bringing its shadowy sword downwards in a great arc. But Stefan and his half-angels scattered just before they were struck, diving in three different directions before meeting again, swords thrust forward.

They pierced the demon in three separate places. The creature screamed and died right there in the sky. It collapsed down into the city in a flaming heap, leaking out oily black blood as it fell. It collapsed into the side of a skyscraper, shattering glass.

Stefan whooped in victory before turning in the sky again. Everywhere he looked, demons were being matched by half-angels swinging flashing, shining blades.

They were winning. He had been prepared to fight until his death, but they were *winning*.

In all of his years fighting for the Holy Order in Rome, he had killed countless minor demons. He had fought alongside half-angels, and they had defeated their enemies at great cost. This was different. This was like heaven had come to Earth. They were an unstoppable force, one that could surely make the holy war history if they concentrated their efforts.

Then there was a change.

Dark clouds seemed to roll out of nowhere, smothering the sun. Simultaneously, the remaining demons gave out a howl that echoed across the city. They began to fight with renewed strength, charging and moving at a terrifying speed.

Stefan saw half-angels falling from the sky: a horrific series of bodies with severed wings, raining blood down onto the city.

What the hell just happened?

He scanned the city, looking for an answer. His gaze settled on the mansion. That city girl had told her that was the place where the portal had been opened.

It was now covered in darkness. It was a darkness that grew and spread, swallowing light as it escaped the building in waves, as though it were alive.

Archangel Michael gave a rallying cry. Stefan charged back toward him, along with every half-angel that was gathered.

"What's going on?" Stefan demanded.

"This darkness is not natural," said Archangel Michael. "Such a sight has not been seen upon this Earth since the days of Ezekiel."

"Speak sense."

"Lucifer has come," said Michael. "The devil walks the Earth and gives strength to his forces. We *must* fight together now, or we will stand no chance."

Stefan's instinct, whenever his authority was questioned, was to argue. But this time he kept his mouth closed.

The demons were approaching them, moving in a flock. He drew his sword and prepared himself to follow Michael's directions.

"We target one demon at a time," said Michael. "Many of you will die, but we cannot slow our pace."

Michael charged, his great sword held high above his head. As he moved, a beam of sunlight broke through the dark clouds, surrounding him. Stefan pushed his fear down deep into his stomach and followed the archangel's lead.

He would fight until he was killed. He had decided that from the moment that he had left his home.

*

Diamond stood still. Her every instinct told her to run, but she couldn't. The devil's eyes were deep blue and spellbinding, impossible to turn away from.

The devil waved a hand, and from the ground behind them burst two great, skeletal arms. They grabbed Barry and Marco and held them tight. A third arm burst through the ground at the entrance of the stairwell away from the basement, blocking it entirely.

Damn, Diamond thought as she looked around her. There was no way to escape. She was a prisoner to Lucifer.

Archangel Michael should never have encouraged them. This was not someone that she could fight, surely.

"I can sense your feelings as well as you can read mine," Lucifer said. "I sense fear in your heart, Diamond. But you don't need to fear a thing. By coming to me, you've chosen the wisest course of action. I can give you everything you ever wanted if you simply help me in return."

"Shut up, creep," said Diamond. She knew it was a weak reply, but it was about all she could manage. Lucifer was taking steps closer. The darkness was behind him, covering the other side of the basement, making it look like a void.

"The half-breeds out there are making my life difficult. But you and I both know they cannot resist for long. The demon spawn upon the Earth right now are just the first wave. Countless demons and Dark Ones are ready to march through my portal. They are a concentrated army that will cover every corner of the Earth, murdering all in their path. But I would rather not let that happen. I need people to serve me; to worship me. I do not wish humanity to suffer. I just want them to understand true power." He smiled. It was a warm smile, almost friendly. Almost believable. "If you can tell me how to defeat these half-angels quickly, then you will make my transition to power quite painless. I know you have spent much time with them, Diamond. I know you have fought alongside them, and you know that their divine blood makes them wayward, lost souls. They have weaknesses, and I wish to know them."

"You talk way too much," said Diamond. She brandished her sword. "Step right back through that portal and go back to where you came from. Earth has enough narcissists without the king of narcissists trying to take control."

Lucifer vanished. When he spoke again, he was inches from her ear. Close enough that Diamond could feel his breath against her cheek.

She was in the void now, surrounded by darkness. There was no floor below her feet and no ceiling above her head. It was just her and Lucifer.

"I know your past," he said. He whispered the words intimately. As soft and gentle as Marco had been when they had spent the night before together. "I know how selfish you've been. I don't judge you at all. Selfishness is just the way that our soul searches for what it wants. The heavens ask so much from you. They've taken your life. Your teenage years have been spent in service to the heavens that have never listened to you.

"I can sense your resistance. I know what you've been told, Diamond. You're fighting against an enemy. Do you feel some obligation to humanity? I would say humanity doesn't deserve someone like you. You've always been an outcast. Even invisible to your own mother. You tried to make it on your own, but they called you a troubled teen. They took away your freedom."

"How do you know all of this?"

"I can know a lot, just from looking into people's eyes. I know you've been hurt, Diamond. I feel sympathy for you, that you've had to handle everything alone. But you don't have to be alone anymore."

When Lucifer spoke, it was like she heard the words in her heart as well as in her ears. Her every instinct told her to listen to him. His voice carried trust, understanding, and something darker and more tempting, as well.

"I can give you the freedom to stop fighting. You don't have to pretend with me, Diamond. You can be the flawed version of yourself. I think flaws are beautiful."

No. Diamond conjured up images of her friends in her head. People who had fought for her. People who had died fighting the same fight she had. People who had sacrificed their safety for hers.

Lucas. Mrs. Delphine. Johnnie. Ida. Marco. Humanity was far from selfish.

"Your friends? Yes, they've done some good for you. But only in return for your help. Never forget how you met these people, Diamond. Taken to a facility, against your will. You were a prisoner."

"I needed help."

"But you didn't ask for help. And that's not all that the world has done to you."

The void around her swirled into color. Diamond saw visions of her past, earlier memories that she'd tried to blank out. Kids at school bullying her. No one at home to protect and console her. Turning her to drink. She had to fight alone all her life, just to survive.

And that anger hadn't gone away entirely. It was always bubbling in the back of her head. It had fueled her when the portal had first opened. It had stopped her from helping. It had made her bitter and depressed.

She didn't want to feel that shame and unworthiness again, but Lucifer dragged it up from the darkest parts of her mind until it was a raging fire.

Then Lucifer showed her a new vision, and it all receded away. She was one of Lucifer's fallen angels, flying with others at her side. They spread around the Earth, conquering city to city. In return, Lucifer gave her power, wealth, and freedom. A chance to do and be anything that she wanted.

There wasn't any anger anymore, just relief. Confidence like she had never known. For once she could turn off her instincts as an empath. She could stop wasting so much energy worrying about others, and she could worry about herself.

"You are at a crossroads in your life, Diamond," said Lucifer. "One road, you can see before you. The other involves war, fire, and death. Probably the death of those you love most. I admire your bravery but admit it. You and your friends cannot overcome the forces of hell. Why die fighting for something when you could join it and be part of the glory?"

Diamond was tempted. More tempted than she had been by anything in her life. The satisfaction of letting go, the ability to stop worrying, to focus on herself, was something she had been quietly waiting for her entire life.

But no. She hadn't spent these years fighting, losing, and suffering just to give up now. Not so close to the end. If Lucifer was bargaining with her, then at least part of him had to recognize that she was a threat.

After all, it had been her prayer that had sent an archangel down to Earth. She'd been the one to rouse the other half-angels in the prison.

"I'm bigger than this," she said. "Bigger than all of these pointless offers. I'm a half-angel, and I'm going to do what I was always meant to do."

She drew her sword and Lucifer's expression changed at once. His bright features twisted into something barely human. His blue eyes turned yellow and his mouth opened, baring teeth.

"You are a waste of life, Diamond," he hissed. "A human pawn, just like the others."

Diamond didn't listen to him anymore. She swung her sword with all of the strength that she could muster, aiming straight for Lucifer's horrible face.

Her blade cut through nothing. It fell into darkness and she tripped, suddenly spinning in the void. Lucifer reappeared about 20 feet away. He raised his hand to the void, and suddenly the darkness became solid. He threw a spear of black matter at her, and Diamond ducked as it sailed over her head. There were more projectiles after that, coming in rapid succession.

Diamond could barely think as she ducked and weaved out of their way. The last one came straight towards her face. She deflected it at the last moment by swinging her sword.

But then she couldn't move. The darkness around her feet swirled into tendrils that held her fast. She strained against their grip, but nothing could move them. She tried to swing her sword, but her arms were restrained, as well.

Lucifer was directly in front of her again, a black dagger in his hands.

"I made you an offer, you fool," he said. "Now I'm going to cut your heart out."

"You're going to return to hell," said a man's voice, full of authority.

Diamond was unexpectedly free. The basement came back into view, suddenly illuminated by white light.

Two archangels stood on either side of her. Like Michael, they wielded huge flaming swords. The one who had spoken had long brown hair that reached down to his shoulders and a youthful, calm expression. He was graceful whereas Michael had been bold. He radiated beauty and calm. Diamond felt an overwhelming sense of relief just being in his presence.

At the sight of the two archangels, Lucifer transformed. His face twisted and elongated. His body lengthened and became wreathed with fire.

Suddenly he was a red dragon. He looked like a snake but had dozens of clawed legs running down the sides of his body, which was scarred, fetid, and wounded. Upon the top of his head were two curved horns, like a mountain goat's, though sharper, hooked, and menacing.

Diamond felt like she was going to hurl. *This* was what she had almost been tempted by?

"Gabriel," said Lucifer. "You have no place here. Even your so-called warrior brother Michael didn't defeat me." He rose high above the archangels, casting them in shadow. He curved each of his fingers and toes, displaying an array of blade-like talons. "I am still here."

"You're a shadow of what you once were. You've spent so long in the darkness you've lost everything that makes you divine. Besides, Raphael and I don't need to defeat you. We only need to seal you."

"No seal can hold me forever!"

"No. But every time you reappear, goodness will prevail. That is why these humans have free will, devil. For all of their faults, they make the right choices in the end."

Before Lucifer could speak again, Gabriel raised his palm. A barrier of light was between him and the devil, and the devil was forced backward toward the portal.

At the same time, Raphael soared to the portal. As the devil passed through the veil of darkness, he struck the portal with his heavenly blade.

The ground shook. The darkness was overwhelmed by light. The stone outline of the portal cracked and crumbled, and then everything was still.

Diamond was panting. Blood was dripping from her limbs, but she was alive. She looked around the basement, finally able to take in all of her surroundings. Barry and Marco looked to be unharmed, as well.

They did it. They sent the beast back to his hell hole.

With some help, admittedly. But still.

"That feels good," she said.

"To be rid of him?" said Marco.

Diamond nodded. "He made me think things that I thought I'd buried forever. But I guess I've got some demons in my head left to slay, as well as out there on the battlefield."

"Now is not the time for discussion," said Raphael. "We have a horde of demon spawn out there in this city to clear."

"I'll lead the way," said Diamond, spreading her wings.

CHAPTER ————————15

"Is it over?" Lucas asked as Diamond sprinted out of the mansion and past him.

"Almost," said Diamond. "You and Ida keep work on the ground. The rest of us have more work to do. Clean up duty."

Lucas and Ida nodded.

Diamond took into the air with two archangels beside her. They charged forward to the city, where the battle seemed to be looking desperate. More desperate than Diamond had feared.

There was just a smattering of half-angels lingering in the sky, and surrounding them were at least a dozen demons. Worse than that, Diamond recognized several skeletal monsters that could only be Dark Ones flying high in the sky through some dark force that couldn't be seen.

But it didn't matter. She'd already slain a Dark One. She'd already faced Lucifer and lived. Plus, they now had a total of three archangels on their side. All three of them wasted no time combining their strength.

They fought in a trio, with Michael leading the charge. The blows of his sword were powerful enough to send demons rocketing towards the ground like falling comets. Gabriel and Raphael met their bodies in their descent, striking at the corpses with sword strikes that brought claps of thunder.

Diamond flew past the work that the three archangels were doing. She joined a small gathering of the remaining half-angels at the far end of the city who were doing their best to try and outpace a single Dark One. As she neared them, Diamond caught a glimpse of Stefan's face. He was scared, and his face was tainted in the same way as Marco's wing had been. He was gasping, barely staying airborne.

As Diamond approached, she healed him. She healed every single wounded half-angel that was gathered there; it came to her as easy as breathing now. Their feelings and their pain came to her in perfect clarity. She was unburdened by her anxiety and worry now. Diamond knew that they would win.

"You're all afraid," she shouted at the half-angels. "I get it. I've been afraid, too. But your fear is holding you back. We *can* fight and win here. They want us to remain imprisoned in our fear and doubt because courage and faith are our greatest weapons. We *can* beat them, but it's going to take the light of all of us to do so."

She met Stefan's eyes as she talked. He nodded at her and then raised his sword.

"The light of all!" he repeated.

"The light of all!" screamed the crowd of half-angels in unison.

What followed next was divine smite. The half-angels fell upon the nearest Dark One in a choreographed dance of battle. With cuts from a dozen light-filled blades, the Dark One's bones crumbled into dust.

The half-angels charged through the sky, wiping out the remaining demons one by one. Some tried to flee, but they were easy to spot and had slowed down now that they didn't have the presence of Lucifer to inspire them.

Diamond and those who fought with her hunted every demon down. Diamond saw a dozen different divine powers, all of which caused a new kind of havoc for their enemies. One half-angel, a young girl with dark skin and fierce eyes, sent out flashes of light that blinded the demons before they reached them, turning each of them into sitting targets that could be cut down with ease.

A guy with red-dyed hair could summon a ball of holy flame that charged through the sky like a deadly pinball. Whenever a demon strayed too close, the ball kept them at bay, striking at them and knocking them back.

An androgynous kid who couldn't be any older than 15 was able to create shields of light that protected others just before they were about to be struck by darkness. Whenever a demon got close enough to strike at someone, the kid would be there, repelling the demon's blows with their divine, impenetrable force.

Diamond watched these little frays as she tackled her enemies, capturing glances of these different powers in action out of the corner of her eye. It was a beautiful sight. All of these kids were probably once wayward souls, just like her. Some of them she recognized as the prisoners that she rescued. But they weren't prisoners in their hearts anymore. They were free, emboldened by the wild spirit that their angelic blood provided them.

She thought back on what Lucifer had said, about how she was always alone. He was right on some counts. She often felt alone, even when she was in a room with all of her friends.

One thing was certain though; she didn't feel alone right now. She didn't know the names of any of these kids who were fighting alongside her, but she felt a deep connection with them in her soul. She knew their feelings and could sense their stories and their pasts. They had regained a little bit of hope, just like she had. Their stories were linked together and were now uniting in a glorious defense of the best parts of humanity.

Diamond was beginning to see—at least a little—why the heavens had been so obsessed with the free will of humanity. Without the desire to pull together and fight, they would never have found the strength that they had that day. Diamond would never have been able to be the leader that she needed to be. She would always be ruled by fear, unable to solve problems for herself. She wasn't sure that excused the deaths that had happened, but who was to say how many more deaths there would have been if they hadn't learned to fight for themselves?

The final Dark One hung over the top of the Wells Fargo center. It had a gigantic ball of flame in its hands. It was threatening to throw it down into the city below.

"Don't step further, or I'll lay waste to this whole damned place!" it howled in a warning.

"No, you won't," said Marco. "You're not fast enough."

The Dark One unleashed the ball of flame. It rocketed towards the city. Marco moved at breakneck speed, slashing the flaming projectile with his holy sword, dispelling the flames.

At the same time, Diamond, Stefan, and a horde of half-angels surrounded the Dark One, blades drawn. She let Stefan finish the battle, cleaving the creature directly down the middle.

*

Diamond touched the ground outside of the building that had once been the shopping mall, but which was now a mess of bullet holes, dead Vipers, and smashed glass. Ida, seeing her, grinned. She approached and put an arm around Diamond's shoulder.

"The LGs stopped fighting when the demons started disappearing," said Ida. "Some of the Vipers kept going, but they aren't so tough when we've got numbers on our side."

Diamond looked around. Ida had succeeded in assembling a small army of people who had come out from hiding to finally fight for what was theirs. They had taken guns from the slain LGs by the looks of it, and now many of them were wandering around the carnage, acting a little lost.

Thankfully, Lucas was there to direct them. Already he was filling Mrs. Delphine's shoes, instructing groups of people to collect blankets and food, and to start fires for those who were wounded or needed extra care. When he caught sight of Diamond, his face was beaming with pride.

"You're far from the girl you were when I first met you," he said. "You've grown up fast, Diamond."

"And it looks like you've managed to finally mature, yourself."

Lucas snorted at that. Then he glanced around the mess that Minneapolis had become. Black smoke still ran down every alley, and the place smelt like a barbecue. Every single street was marred with scorch marks, and there were piles of trash on every corner.

"This is a new challenge," he said. "Can't say I know much about putting a city back together."

"There will be people who know. You should let them get to it, Lucas. We've done our job."

Lucas shook his head. "Mrs. Delphine wouldn't take a step back, even if she was out of her depths. I'll try and get the ball rolling on things, at least. We'll need a good shelter for everybody, for a start."

Together they stood in quiet for a few moments. Then Diamond asked a nervous question that was starting to play on her mind.

"Do you think that's the end of it now?" she asked.

"I'm not sure. We've never had a victory like this before. Or anything close to this level of battle. However, demon kind, and the people that follow them, don't give up easily. But don't worry about that now, Diamond. For now, you can rest."

Diamond nodded. She couldn't remember the last time that she properly rested, without any worries and troubles playing on her mind. For once, she felt like she could go down to sleep peacefully.

CHAPTER ––––––––16

Spring came warm that year, which was good for everyone's spirits. As Diamond gathered with the others around the front steps of the old rehab building, there was a smell of blossom in the air. There was sunshine on her skin, too, punctuated by a refreshing breeze.

"It's a good day for fresh starts," Marco said, shuffling next to her and squeezing her hand.

"The best we could ask for," said Diamond. But she couldn't quite return his smile.

At the top of the steps, Lucas tapped a microphone. It buzzed, and the crowd fell to silence.

Diamond spent some time studying the scene around her. It was crazy to think that just a few months earlier, it would have been an impossible gathering. Half-angels stood with their wings extended alongside city officials, the mayor, and several other experts in the fields of health and psychology.

The secret of angels was out of the bottle now and, for now at least, the world had been very accepting of their semi-divine society members. More than that, they were treated like heroes. Diamond was beginning to find it a little embarrassing to be offered free meals every time she wandered down a city street. Even worse than that were the people asking for autographs. She had given in a couple of times to the request, but every time she did it made her cringe so hard she just wanted to vanish.

"It's been a dark year for the world. But a particularly dark year for Minneapolis," said Lucas. As he spoke, Diamond could see him emulating snatches of Mrs. Delphine's oration style.

He talked from deep in his chest and took the time to meet the eyes of the people gathered to listen.

It made Diamond smile. Lucas honored their fallen friend every day. He kept her memory alive in the way that he carried the lessons and skills she had left.

Lucas continued. "The city will never quite be the same as it was, but we should be proud of what we've all been able to achieve in such a short space of time. People in Minneapolis have electricity again, thanks to the solar generators we've helped to build. We have good sources of water, and good connections to other, less affected cities across the country. There are imports of food, new businesses opening every day, and people are out on the streets, laughing and coming together.

"But one issue that has not been addressed is the issue of half-angels walking among us. I know they are revered as heroes, but there are other half-angels out there. Other kids who have no idea that they have a divine heritage. For these kids, life is going to be hard. They need a place where they can go and thrive, and learn how to manage their gifts. Now that the existence of angels has become public knowledge, I believe that it's time we take our rehabilitation programs a step further. This is why I am honored to announce the grand opening of the newly refurbished Angel's Haven—now renamed the Delphine Institute for Angelic Restoration!"

He gave a nod, and a young winged girl pulled off a sheet of fabric that was concealing a statue. Even though Diamond knew that Lucas had gotten it commissioned, seeing the finished product still brought a lump to her throat.

Mrs. Delphine's statue was perfect. Even though it was cast in bronze, it still somehow caught the sharp glare in her eyes. Every angle of her face was etched in concern, but with warmth, as well. It was exactly as Diamond remembered her.

"Our new institute will do more than just rehabilitate troubled teens," said Lucas. "We will also help half-angels to integrate into society. We will show them how they can use their powers to contribute to the world. That could be through fighting, or it could be helping in society or industry. Our goal is to provide half-angels with a guiding light when they have no one else that they can turn to."

An enthusiastic rattle of applause followed Lucas's speech. Glancing around, Diamond saw that she wasn't the only one there with tears in her eyes. Many of the other half-angels looked emotional, as well, even though many of them had nothing to do with Angel's Haven or Mrs. Delphine.

Diamond knew what they were all thinking. They were considering what a dream a place like this would have been to them during their wayward, younger days. It was a huge emotional relief to know that things didn't need to be carried out in secret anymore. It would make helping the half-angels of the world so much easier.

*

As the event wound down and people began to peel away from the celebration, Diamond joined a small gathering of the people she cared about most. They stood on the pleasant grounds of the Delphine Institute, near a newly installed fountain that gently trickled as they smiled and laughed.

Only Johnnie was quiet. Ever since the day they had won the battle for Minneapolis, his mood had hardly changed at all. He always seemed to be looking at something that the others couldn't see. His brow was almost always furled, like he was trying to figure out some great problem in the future.

"Relax for a day, little brother," Marco told him, putting a hand on his shoulder. "Hasn't this whole mess taught you to enjoy the here and now? We've got a peaceful day today, with friends. Who knows when we'll get another one?"

"You're not a medicine man. It isn't so easy," said Johnnie.

"The fighting's over."

"It's never over, Marco. We are in an era of peace right now, but no era lasts forever. The war between heaven and hell has been raging since ancient days, and it will continue to progress long after we die. Good and evil are always out of balance in humanity, and Lucifer knows it. He's biding his time, waiting for the moment that he can act again, to try and capture the hearts of the selfish."

"He's right," said Diamond. "Our work isn't done."

Marco raised an eyebrow at her. Diamond quickly looked down at her feet. There was something that she had been meaning to tell him; something that she had been putting off for a long time. She wasn't sure how he was going to take it. It irritated her. After all this time, after everything she had learned, she was still avoiding difficult conversations.

She waited until Lucas returned and the conversation in the group turned to more trivial matters. Ida talked about her new girlfriend. Lucas talked about the vacation he had planned. Diamond gave Marco a knowing look and didn't have to say anything. Quietly they slipped away, around the back of the rehab center, to talk in private.

To Diamond, he had never looked more attractive. He had grown a lot, carrying himself with the confidence and purpose of someone who knew what his role was in life. He had worked hard alongside Lucas to get the Delphine Institute up and running. He had drawn from his own experiences as a half-angel and had implemented several programs and initiatives designed to give them more freedom and choice about their treatment and what they wanted to get out of the program.

"I'm proud of you. I haven't had a chance to say it, since we've both been so busy," said Diamond.

"We haven't been alone since that night in the tent."

"You almost managed to say that without blushing."

"Almost," said Marco, smiling. "But I'm guessing you haven't brought me back here so we can have another night together. You've got that 'I've got bad news face' on."

Diamond returned his smile. "I've been talking to Barry—I mean, to my dad. Lucas has offered us both jobs here, but he thinks we can do more good out in the world. The world is bigger than Minneapolis, and who knows how many half-angels out there need help?"

"You never were good at staying in one place for long."

"You're staying here, aren't you?"

Marco nodded slowly. "Lucas has some brilliant ideas, but he doesn't know what it's like to be a half-angel. He's offered me the position of co-director. I don't know what that means, but I know I can help. Besides, someone has to be here to keep an eye on Johnnie."

They were quiet for a while after that. A gentle breeze moved the grass around their feet. They watched the birds fluttering in and out of the hedgerows, stopping once and a while to meet each other's eyes.

"This is the hardest and easiest goodbye I've ever had to say," said Diamond, eventually.

"That's because it isn't goodbye. No matter where you end up Diamond, I'm going to be here. I've got a love for you that can't break, and we've been through too much together now to forget that. You do whatever you need to do, and I'll do the same. One day we might end up back in the same place—who knows?" He held her hand, grasping it tight. "All I know is you've got my heart. Whenever you're ready to let others pick up the fight, I'll be right here. We can go and have another night under the stars."

They kissed then. It was gentle—a shadow of the passion they had mustered before. Diamond felt like the kiss was a promise. A marker that one day, whenever they were both ready, they'd pick things back up exactly how they left them.

She could see inside his heart. She knew that the trust and love he felt for her was pure and real. No matter what she went through from now on, she'd always have someone she could turn to for comfort.

*

Diamond got into the passenger seat of Barry's new car. She looked out at the Delphine Institute; at the building that had been part of her life for so long. When she thought back to the girl who had arrived here, a troubled teen with nowhere to go, it was like thinking about someone else.

Angel's Haven had done its job. She felt rehabilitated. She felt like she had gained the courage and skills she needed to make the most of her life.

"Where to first?" she asked.

"Wherever we're needed," said Barry. He had never quite lost the spark he had gained following the arrival of the archangels. His voice didn't have a sarcastic edge anymore. Barry said what he meant, and he was more determined than anyone to help out others. "Perhaps it's time that we found your mom back in the city. I knew her before all of these terrible things happened to her. The woman I knew wouldn't have liked the woman she's become."

Diamond took a deep breath. Facing her mom again was terrifying, especially after how they had left things last. Since the Battle of Minneapolis, she had heard that her mom was still in the city. She was one last reminder of Diamond's past. But it was a reminder that Diamond didn't want to ignore any longer.

"Lead the way, dad," she said.

Barry put the car into drive and started the engine. As they drove off through the tree-lined highway, Diamond didn't look back once at the Delphine Institute. Her mission was ahead now. It was time to put the fight behind her.

Now it was time to look ahead to a better future. For her, and for all half-angel kids like her, who were suffering with no one looking out for them.